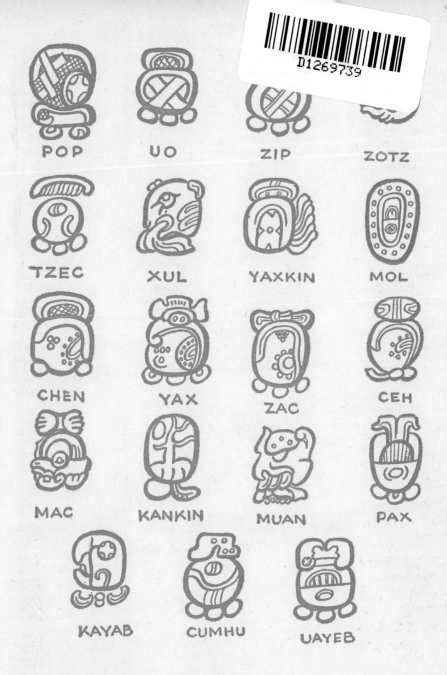

POP UO ZIP ZOTZ

TZEC XUL YAXKIN MOL

CHEN YAX ZAC CEH

MAC KANKIN MUAN PAX

KAYAB CUMHU UAYEB

Name-glyphs of the eighteen Maya months, including the five-day unlucky
Uayeb period.

The Happy Hollisters and the Mystery of the Mexican Idol

BY JERRY WEST

Illustrated by Helen S. Hamilton

GARDEN CITY, NEW YORK

DOUBLEDAY & COMPANY, INC.

Endpapers by Alberto Beltrán. Reprinted from World of the Maya *by Victor von Hagen (New American Library of World Literature), by permission of Lester Lewis Associates.*

Contents

CHAPTER 1

A NEW TOY

"Will it bite me?" asked little Sue Hollister.

"Yikes!" replied redheaded Ricky. "How can a toy snake bite anybody?"

"Especially," chimed in Holly, twirling one of her pigtails, "if it's purple with yellow spots and has a smiling face!"

The two sisters, four and six years old, and their brother, who was seven, were looking into the window of a toy shop at the airport a few miles outside of Shoreham, their home town. It was an exciting afternoon for the whole family, including Mother and Daddy and Pete and Pam, because Uncle Russ Hollister was coming from the West Coast with a big secret.

Dark-haired Sue, who loved secrets, kept her bright eyes on the long velvety cotton snake. "Oh, I wish we could have her!" she said.

"How do you know the snake's a *her?*" asked Ricky, wrinkling his freckled nose.

"'Cause her name is Mathilda," replied the younger girl.

"And how do you know that?" asked Holly.

"'Cause I named her that already," declared Sue. "Don't you think Mathilda is a good name?"

5

Just then the two other Hollister children walked up. Pete was a handsome twelve-year-old boy with a crew cut. Pam, two years younger, had fluffy golden hair and a happy smile.

"We all like Mathilda," Ricky said, pointing to the snake in the window. "Do you 'spose we could buy her?"

"Crickets!" said Pete. "That would be great fun to have. How much does she cost?" The boy pressed closer to the glass in order to see the price tag. It was marked six dollars.

"I've only got thirty-nine cents," said Ricky, jiggling a few coins in his pocket. The other children counted what money they had, and it made a grand total of three dollars and sixty-two cents.

Suddenly they heard a voice behind them. "So there you are!"

The children whirled about to see their father smiling at them. He was a tall, handsome man wearing light blue slacks and a sport shirt to match.

"We wondered where you had disappeared," he said.

"Oh, Daddy, we'd like to buy Mathilda," Pam said.

"Who's Mathilda?" he asked and was quickly told. When he learned how much extra money was needed to purchase the snake, Mr. Hollister went inside the shop with his children. The clerk took Mathilda from the window and handed her to Sue. After everyone helped to pay, they left the shop, smiling happily. Sue tucked the snake's head under her arm and Ricky draped the back end over his shoulder.

"What kind of snake is she?" asked Sue, as they trooped across the terminal floor toward the ticket counter, where her mother waited.

"It's a *spotted purple friendly*," replied Daddy. "I think Mother will be surprised to see it."

"Oh, dear, what do you have there?" exclaimed Mrs. Hollister as the children ran up to her. She was a slender, blond woman with blue eyes.

"It's a spotted purple friendly named Mathilda," explained Sue. "Here, pet her, Mommy."

As Mrs. Hollister bent down to pet the velvety nose, an announcement came over the public address system.

"Passengers awaiting flight sixty-three from Los Angeles to New York: there may be a delay in departure from this airport due to an emergency aboard this flight."

"That's the plane Uncle Russ is on," said Pam with a startled look.

"What's the trouble?" Mr. Hollister asked the clerk behind the counter.

"I really don't know, sir. The aircraft is just landing now."

Hearing this, Ricky and Holly dashed toward stairs which led to an observation deck overlooking the airfield. The others hastened after them with Sue dragging Mathilda along behind her.

A strong wind whipped their hair as the children pressed close to the railing to watch the plane taxi in. All at once, a small white truck sped across the field. It stopped near the big aircraft and two men jumped out with nets in their hands.

"Oh, dear," said Holly. "Perhaps someone on the plane is dangerous!"

"Or maybe a wild animal is loose," was Pete's guess.

When the plane was still some distance from the terminal building, a portable stairway was rolled up to it. The front door opened and the two men with nets hastened aboard. For a few minutes the Hollisters watched the open doorway anxiously. Then passengers began to step out of the airplane.

"Look, there's Uncle Russ!" Ricky shrieked, as a tall, broad-shouldered man started lightly down the long flight of stairs.

"Come on!" Holly shouted and raced through the terminal toward the loading gate, with the other children pell-mell behind her.

Their hearts pounded with excitement, for they adored their fun-loving uncle, who visited them every chance he had on his trips between the East and West Coasts. He was a famous cartoonist, who drew comic strips for a chain of newspapers.

"A live snake?" asked Pam.

Uncle Russ lived in the town of Crestwood with Aunt Marge and their two children Teddy and Jean.

As the Hollisters dashed through the loading gate

onto the field, they saw him pause to look over the white truck.

"Uncle Russ! Uncle Russ, what happened?" Ricky said, scrambling into his uncle's arms.

Sue, whose chubby legs were not as long as the others', trotted beside her mother, with Mathilda looped around her neck. Uncle Russ saw the stuffed snake and his eyes widened.

"Well, what do you know about that! A snake caused the trouble on our airplane."

"I'll say it was!" the cartoonist replied. "The thing slithered all over the cabin. Everyone was in a panic!"

"I would imagine so," said Mrs. Hollister. "Did it bite anyone?"

"Fortunately no. But in the excitement, I lost my briefcase."

"Was your secret in it?" Holly spoke up. She remembered a telephone call from her uncle the day before when he told them he was bringing a secret to Shoreham.

Uncle Russ patted his breast pocket. "No. I put the secret in my wallet, thank goodness."

As he spoke, the two men with the nets hastened past them, followed by a crowd of onlookers.

"Well, we caught it all right," one of them said. His net was bulging with a long snake the color of golden corn.

"A seven-footer!" exclaimed the other attendant and added, "There was a professor on the plane.

9

He identified the snake as a Cribo. It comes from the jungles of Yucatán."

Uncle Russ's eyebrows shot up. "Yucatán?" he asked. He shook his head and said nothing further, as he went to claim his baggage.

Afterward, he reported the loss of the briefcase to the ticket counter. The clerk promised that a search would be made immediately and jotted down the Hollisters' phone number.

With the suitcase tucked safely in the back of their station wagon, the family set off for home. As they passed cars on the way, Ricky waggled Mathilda's head out the window to make people laugh.

"That Cribo snake being from Yucatán is a very odd coincidence," Uncle Russ said.

"You mean your secret is about Yucatán?" Pam asked.

"That's right," said Uncle Russ.

"Where's Yucatán?" asked Ricky.

"It's a peninsula in southern Mexico," Pam replied. "We studied about it in school. The Maya Indians live there."

"Are there Indians in your secret?" Holly asked wide-eyed.

Uncle Russ grinned. "Only one—so far."

"Oh, please tell us all about it," Holly pleaded.

"Wait till I catch my breath. That Cribo really gave me a bad scare!" her uncle replied.

Finally Mr. Hollister pulled into the long driveway leading to their home. The house, old-fashioned and rambling, was set in the middle of wide lawns and the back yard, shaded by two weeping willows, ran right into Pine Lake.

Zip, the Hollisters' collie dog, bounded from behind the house and trotted up to lick Sue's hand as she scrambled out of the car, cradling Mathilda in her arms like a baby.

Pete carried his uncle's suitcase to the guest room, while Pam hastened to the kitchen to prepare a pitcher of lemonade. When she served it on the porch, Uncle Russ said, "Hm, that tastes good! Has it been pretty hot here this summer?"

"Too hot," his brother said. "Look at that brown lawn. We haven't had any rain for three weeks."

"You're not on good terms with the rain god," their guest replied with a wink. Then he added quickly, "Now I'll tell you my secret."

Sue Hollister climbed into his lap and Ricky straddled the porch railing beside him as the others crowded around.

"I have a friend named Skeets Packer," Uncle Russ began. "He's sort of an oddball—an archeologist and photographer."

"An arche—what?" asked Ricky, scratching his head.

"You know what an archeologist is," said Pam. "He discovers old ruins and learns about ancient history that way."

"Sh-sh," declared Sue impatiently. "We want to hear the secret."

11

Uncle Russ continued. "Well, about two years ago my friend Skeets discovered a Mayan temple pyramid in the jungles of Yucatán."

"Oh boy!" Ricky said. "Jungles are great!"

"This one," Uncle Russ went on, "is very wild, and the temple is so old that it's of great historic value." He explained that Skeets Packer had photographed part of it, but had never let anybody know the location.

"Why?" asked Holly.

"Because treasure hunters might find the place and steal all the ancient things out of it."

"What a wonderful secret!" said Mrs. Hollister. "Are there many such temples in Yucatán, Russ?"

"Oh, yes, dozens of them," he said, "and too many people have been stealing the contents before the Mexican Government can preserve them."

He said that Skeets had named his discovery the *Temple of the Laughing Idol*, because there was a grinning stone figure standing before it.

Pete spoke up. "So now what is your friend going to do?"

"Skeets Packer is ill," Uncle Russ said, "and is resting in a mountain resort in California. I saw him there just the other day. He gave me a map showing how to find the old temple pyramid."

"Are you going there, Uncle Russ?" Pam asked.

"That's the idea." He reached into his wallet and pulled out a map. "I'm going to find the place, make sketches for my newspaper strip, then turn all the information over to the Mexican Government. And," he added, looking from one child to the other, "your Aunt Marge and Jean and Teddy are in Chichén Itzá waiting for me with a Mayan guide named Balám. He's the Indian I mentioned."

Ricky jumped off the porch rail. "Yikes! Are Teddy and Jean going into the jungle with you?"

"Yes. I think it'll be great fun for them."

"May we go too?" begged Holly.

"That would be the greatest ever!" declared Pete, as his parents exchanged glances.

Their uncle told them more about Chichén Itzá, which was the name of a town where important temple discoveries had been made. "Near it is a big well called a cenote," their uncle said, "and in ancient times, when there was no rain, young maidens were thrown in it as a sacrifice to the rain gods."

Ricky glanced up at the hot bright blue sky and his eyes were dreamy with an idea. He hummed a little tune under his breath, paying no attention to the rest of the conversation.

After Pam had taken the empty lemonade glasses to the kitchen, she and Pete dug several books from a set of encyclopedias and began to read more about Yucatán.

Holly and Sue, meanwhile, followed Ricky to the dock behind their home. "You know Holly, we do need rain badly," said Ricky, cocking his head.

His younger sister caught on immediately. "Are you thinking about sacrificing somebody?"

13

"Well," said Ricky, pressing his chin against his throat in order to look very important, "how about sacrificing a maiden in Pine Lake cenote?"

"Like who?"

"Like *you!*" Ricky said. He pulled Holly toward him by one of her pigtails and pushed her off the dock.

Splash!

Sunsuit and all, Holly disappeared below the surface, then popped up spluttering and swam to shore.

"Ricky, you old meanie!" she yelled.

"Here, here, what's going on?" called Mrs. Hollister at the back door.

"I got sacrificed!" shouted Holly and waded dripping onto the back lawn.

"Oh, that Ricky!" Mrs. Hollister said, as the pigtailed girl dripped into the house, and up to her room for a change of clothes.

"I'm next!" piped up little Sue, but Ricky stood at the dock, openmouthed, as he gazed into the sky. A big, gray cloud swept across Pine Lake and blotted out the sun. He raced into the house with Sue at his heels to tell Pete and Pam what had happened.

Five minutes later, when Holly came down in a dry dress, ominous rumbling sounded from across the lake. This was followed by thunder and lightning.

"Good night!" declared Pete. "It really worked!"

"I got sacrificed!" shouted Holly.

"You know that's impossible," said Pam. "It had to rain sooner or later!"

At the height of the storm, as Uncle Russ sat in the living room chuckling over the strange coincidence, the telephone rang. Pete hastened to answer it, then called, "Long distance for you from California, Uncle Russ!"

The cartoonist moved quickly to the telephone. "Oh, Skeets, it's you. How's everything in California?" Then the cartoonist's face wrinkled in a frown. He listened for a few minutes, then said, "Okay. I'll watch my step. Thanks, Skeets."

"What's the matter, Russ?" Mr. Hollister said.

"Bad news, John. Skeets Packer thinks I'm being followed by a crook!"

CHAPTER 2

A SKULL WARNING

THUNDER boomed, and jagged yellow lightning flashed in the sky. Rain beat down harder than ever, but the Hollisters did not notice. They were gazing at one another in amazement over the telephone call.

"You're being followed!" Pete exclaimed. "What makes Skeets think that?"

"His apartment in Los Angeles has been broken into." Uncle Russ said that old Mayan coins had been stolen, along with photographs which Skeets had taken of Chichén Itzá and other places in Yucatán.

"Skeets thinks the burglar was looking for his map showing how to get to the Temple of the Laughing Idol."

"But how would the thief know you had it, Russ?" Mrs. Hollister asked.

"Skeets returned home from the resort today," he replied, "and discovered that his apartment had been robbed while he was gone. When the burglar didn't find the map, he may have traced Skeets to the resort."

"And spied on both of you!" Pete said, snapping his fingers.

"Exactly," Uncle Russ replied. "He might have heard us talk about my trip to Yucatán and followed me to get hold of the map."

Pam looked puzzled. "But how would anyone in Los Angeles know Skeets had the map?"

Her uncle explained that someone had attempted to steal the map from the archeologist the day before he had left Yucatán. "Skeets said a thin, swarthy man held him up on a deserted street and demanded that he hand it over. But Skeets started fighting and yelling and the fellow ran away."

"Now your friend thinks the man traced him to Los Angeles?" Pam asked.

Uncle Russ nodded.

Pete gave a low whistle. "That thief must want the map pretty bad."

"Yikes!" Ricky said, "there must be plenty of treasure in that temple."

"Very likely," Uncle Russ replied, "since nobody has ever explored it before."

John Hollister asked his brother if he had noticed anybody suspicious on the airplane.

"There was a thin, swarthy man sitting across the aisle one seat to the rear," Russ replied. "He kept staring at me."

"Did the fellow get off in Shoreham?" Pete asked.

"I don't know."

"Well, I think we ought to find out," said Pam anxiously.

"Now don't be a worrywart," said Uncle Russ

with a smile. "Skeets isn't positive the thief is after me. As for the man on the plane—he may have nothing to do with it. Let's just wait and see what happens."

By now the rain had let up and thunder echoed in the distance as the storm passed beyond Shoreham.

While there were still a few sprinkles coming down, the Hollister children kicked off their shoes and ran barefoot through the puddles in their yard.

"Yikes, this is great!" Ricky said, trying to make splashes bigger than anybody else.

Sue went back into the house and returned with Mathilda. "She wants to play too," the little girl said.

"Let's make believe she's a boa constrictor and hang her in a tree," said Pete. He took the snake and flung her over the branch of a maple tree and let her hang there, head down.

Just then a loud voice called, "Hey, look what I've got!"

The children turned to see a tall husky boy of Pete's age coming toward them.

"Here's trouble," muttered Ricky. It was Joey Brill, the neighborhood bully. He was leading a large spotted dog on a piece of heavy rope. The skinny animal had big floppy feet and a bushy tail.

"See my bodyguard," said Joey. "His name's Tiger."

"Where'd you get him?" asked Pete.

"I found him. He's a stray. Watch out—he's fierce."

Pam gazed into the dog's sad eyes. "He doesn't look fierce."

"Don't let him fool you," Joey warned. "He's got bloodhound blood in him. In fact, he's almost pedigreed."

Ricky snorted. "Pedigreed mongrel, you mean."

Joey scowled and glanced at the purple snake. "What's that stupid thing?"

As he spoke the dog growled at the toy and suddenly yanked free. He leaped high, pulled the snake from the tree and streaked across the lawn dragging it behind him.

As Sue screamed and Holly made a dive for Mathilda, Zip came running around the corner of the house. Barking excitedly, he joined the chase, grabbed the snake's tail and began to run the other way.

"Zip! Drop it!" Ricky shouted as the snake stretched taut. Too late! *Ri-ip!* Out popped bits of stuffing!

Pete collared Zip and made him let go, while Pam caught the other dog and coaxed the toy from his jaws.

"Mathilda," sobbed Sue. "Her tummy is torn."

"It's only a seam, honey," said Pam. "We can fix it." She curled up the snake and put it in Sue's arms.

Out popped bits of stuffing.

Joey smirked. "It just shows what you know about dogs. I told you he was fierce. Sic 'em, Tiger, sic 'em!" He pointed toward Pam.

Tiger walked over to the girl and licked her hand. She patted his head. As the Hollisters laughed, Joey picked up the rope and yanked the dog after him.

"You think you're funny," he called as he left. "I'll show you!"

Quickly Pam gathered the pieces of stuffing. Then, taking her little sister by the hand, she went into the house, got a needle and thread from her mother's sewing basket and began to stitch up the snake.

Holly, meanwhile, had raced off to the dock. After the storm, the lake had become quiet and mirrorlike. She knelt on hands and knees and gazed into the water.

"Oh, Ricky," she called to her brother. "Come over here, quick! I see the funniest face in the water!"

"Where?" asked Ricky, bouncing onto the dock like a rubber ball.

"Down there," said Holly. Ricky bent over, his hands touching his ankles.

"Where? I don't see anything?"

"There!"

"That's me I'm looking at!" the boy said, glancing at his reflection. "I'm not funny—"

Holly had risen slowly, and with an impish grin, gave her brother a little push.

"Ow—"

Splash—glub! Ricky tumbled into the lake. A moment later his streaming head popped up. Holly, brushing her hands together, said, "Now we're even, Ricky." With a chuckle she added, "In Shoreham, we sacrifice boys, too."

When her brother swam to the shore, he sneaked up the back stairs to change his wet clothes, not wanting anyone to see him and ask questions.

"Yikes," he muttered. "Fooled by a girl!"

Shortly after, at the dinner table, Mrs. Hollister remarked how clean Ricky looked and how neatly his hair was combed. The redhead merely glanced at Holly, then dug into the plate of Irish stew steaming in front of him.

Conversation quickly turned to Uncle Russ's mystery and where the briefcase could be now. The answer came just as they finished dessert, when the telephone rang. It was the airline calling from New York. The missing case had been found in a corner of the plane when it landed at Kennedy Airport.

"They're sending the briefcase back here on the next flight," Uncle Russ reported. "It'll arrive at eight o'clock."

"Maybe the case was just mislaid during the confusion," Mrs. Hollister said hopefully.

Pam shook her head. "I think that man took it and threw it away when he found the map was not inside."

"I agree with Pam," said Uncle Russ. "Anyway,"

he added cheerfully, "soon I'll have it back and then I'll show you a photograph of the Temple of the Laughing Idol."

Holly's eyes sparkled. "What does the idol look like? Is he real big and scary?"

"With a million teeth?" added Ricky. "Like this?" He stuck his fingers in the corners of his mouth and pulled his lips wide in a fierce grin.

"Ugh," said Pam. "That's horrible. Maybe he's laughing in a nice way."

"I bet he isn't!" declared Ricky. "Tell us, Uncle Russ—is he ugly?"

The cartoonist laughed and rumpled Ricky's hair. "You'll see!"

Holly gave a happy wriggle. "I can't wait!"

In spite of the fact that Sue was sleepy-eyed, all the Hollisters including Zip got into the station wagon and rode to the airport. The plane from New York had landed, and a messenger quickly brought the briefcase to Uncle Russ in the terminal building.

"Thank you so much," the cartoonist said.

"Not at all," replied the messenger. "You'd better see if anything is missing."

As the children watched, Uncle Russ opened the briefcase and checked the contents. Then he gasped. "Yes, something *is* missing—the photo of the Laughing Idol."

In its place was a piece of paper, and Uncle

Russ looked at it. He let out a low whistle, then held up the sketch of a skull.

"Crickets!" Pete said. "That's a warning, Uncle Russ."

"You'd better not go to Yucatán," put in Ricky.

"But you'll have to," Holly said worriedly. "Your children are there!"

"Holly's right," Uncle Russ said. "I must go." Then he added, "But this is a warning, I'm afraid. The skull is very much like the ones carved on a rock in Chichén Itzá near the Temple of Kukulcan."

"Kukulcan!" Pam exclaimed. "We read about that this afternoon." Seeing Holly's puzzled expression, she explained that it was one of the finest examples of a restored Mayan temple.

The airline messenger, meanwhile, told Uncle Russ that his company would do all it could to find out what had happened to the missing photograph.

The Hollisters left for home once more, their minds filled with worry over the warning.

Suddenly Pam spoke up. "We should have asked at the airline office if the thin man got off the plane here."

"That's right," said her father. "We'll call up as soon as we get home."

It was dark by the time they turned into the driveway, still wet from the afternoon's downpour. As they pulled in, Mrs. Hollister let out a startled exclamation. "Look! A light in the guest room! Russ, did you leave it on when we left?"

"Sure didn't!"

"Then somebody's been in the place," Mr. Hollister said. He stopped the car, opened the back door and Zip dashed out. The dog raced around to the rear of the house and the children's father hurried to the front door.

"Hey, it's been jimmied open!" he said. With the men in the lead, they all ran upstairs to the guest room. Mr. Hollister flung the door open and the family gasped at the sight before them.

"Crickets! It looks like a bomb hit this place!" Pete cried out.

CHAPTER 3

A KEEN CLUE

THE ROOM was a shambles. Even Russ's suitcase had been torn open and the lining stripped from it.

"Somebody's still looking for that map," Uncle Russ said.

"And I'll bet it's that thin man!" exclaimed Ricky.

A sudden thought struck Pam. "Oh!" she gasped. "The prowler may still be in our house."

"Come on, then, we'll all search. But be careful," Mr. Hollister said.

Ricky let Zip in the back screen door, and, with the dog barking from room to room, the Hollisters searched the house thoroughly. Last of all they went to the basement, where White Nose, their cat, lay cuddled in a big box with her five kittens.

"White Nose, did you see a burglar?" asked Holly.

The mother cat sat up, stretched, arched her back and with a gentle purring, rubbed her head against Holly's leg.

"She says no," Holly declared.

Pete checked the cellar door, which was still locked, and the family decided that the thief had made a clean getaway.

"We'd better call the police," Mrs. Hollister advised as they climbed the basement stairs into their kitchen.

"I wonder if Officer Cal is on duty tonight," said Pete. He went to the telephone and dialed headquarters. After telling the desk sergeant what had happened, he asked if their friend Cal Newberry was on duty that night.

"Yes, he is," came the reply. "He's out in a prowl car. We'll send him right over."

Cal Newberry, the young policeman, who often helped the Hollisters solve their mysteries, drove quietly up to the house a few minutes later. Pete and Pam were waiting to greet him, and they all went inside, Cal bringing his fingerprint kit.

When he had been told what had happened, the policeman checked doorknobs and other shiny surfaces, but he found only the Hollisters' own prints.

"He wore gloves, like on TV," little Sue said, stifling a yawn. She rubbed her eyes sleepily and added, "I'm going upstairs, Mommy. If you need me, I'll be in bed."

Smiling, Mrs. Hollister kissed the little girl good night. The older children were too excited to think of sleep.

"Come on, maybe we can find some clues outside, Cal," Pete suggested. The policeman got his big flashlight and, with the four youngsters trailing behind him, swept the beam back and forth over the yard. Nothing. But then the policeman searched the road in front of the house. He stopped short just past the driveway. "Oh, oh, look at this!"

"Tire tracks!" declared Pete. "A car was parked here."

"And the tracks point toward the airport," said Holly excitedly.

The searchers hurried back to report what they had found. Then Uncle Russ told Officer Cal his whole story.

"Let's check on the thin man now," said the policeman. "I'll call the airline."

Since Uncle Russ remembered his seat number, it did not take long to identify the passenger referred to.

"His name is Aguila—Quinto Aguila," the airline reported. "Yes, he did get off at Shoreham. Half an hour ago he boarded a flight to New York."

Officer Cal made notes of all the information, then said he would follow up the case as far as the Shoreham angle was concerned.

When he had left, Pam hastened to the bookshelf. "Let's look up more about Yucatán."

"Please, not now," Mrs. Hollister said. "It's so late, and you've had a long and exciting day."

Soon the Hollister house was all dark except for the moonlight which silvered the rooftop.

In the middle of the night a *thump* awakened Pete. He sat up quickly in his bed and listened. "Crickets!" he thought, "there's something downstairs!"

He got up quietly, felt for his slippers, and tiptoed to the stairs. A dim light was coming from the living room.

Pete decided to take a peek before he called his father. He tried the first step. It creaked a little, but he descended the rest as quietly as a cat. Then he drew in a deep breath and said:

"Pam! What are you doing down here?"

On the floor near the bookcase, poring over an encyclopedia by the glow of her flashlight, sat Pam.

"Pete!" she said. "You frightened me!"

"And you scared me, too!" said Pete.

"I had the books all stacked up and they fell over," Pam said. "I'm sorry. It's so interesting," she said as she put the books away.

At breakfast next morning Pam said, "Did you know that the old Mayans had twenty days to a month?"

"No," said Uncle Russ. "How many months were there in a year?"

"Eighteen," she replied. "And you should hear the names of some of them! Pop, Mol, Zac, Mac."

Holly burst into giggles. "You mean it?"

"Sure. And each one has a little picture that stands for it—that's called a glyph." Pam grinned. "There's even one month named Zip."

Pete chuckled. "That glyph should be a picture of our dog."

"Yikes! Twenty days a month," said Ricky. "Time went awfully fast, didn't it?"

"Pete, you frightened me!"

Mrs. Hollister figured quickly in her head, and said, "That makes three hundred and sixty days. What about the other five days in the year?"

"Ha, I'm glad you asked me that," said Pam. "Those were called the unlucky days."

"Like yesterday," Uncle Russ said, as he placed his napkin on the table and pushed back his chair. As he rose from the table, there was a twinkle in his eye. "I was thinking last night," he said, "that the Yucatán trip may be too dangerous for your Aunt Marge and the children."

"But you can't call it off," Ricky said stoutly. "Hollisters don't give up, do they, Daddy?"

Mr. Hollister smiled and his brother said, "That's the spirit. You're right, Redhead."

"I think the best thing to do," said Pete eagerly, "is for us to join you in Yucatán. There's safety in numbers."

The grown-ups laughed and the children's father said, "We knew you'd say that, so we've already talked it over."

The children read the good news in their parents' faces. "You mean we can go?" cried Pam.

"Yes," said Mrs. Hollister. "You'll learn a lot from the trip."

The children whooped and danced around the table like wild Indians.

"We'll be jungle scouts," said Ricky, fighting his way through imaginary vines.

"Are you going, Mommy?" asked Sue, taking her hand.

"Of course," said Mrs. Hollister with a smile. "I'm as good a jungle scout as anybody."

"How'll we get there?" asked Holly.

"Just like Teddy, Jean, and Aunt Marge, I guess," replied their uncle. He explained that they were flown down by an airplane owned by the newspaper syndicate. "I'll see if I can arrange it." He explained that he had to go to New York first on business.

"But what about the map you're carrying?" Pete said. "Do you suppose Aguila will try to steal it again?"

"I'll fool him," Uncle Russ replied. He reached into his wallet, pulled out the map and gave it to Pete. "Nobody would think of finding it on you. Will you keep it safe for me?"

"You bet I will," Pete declared. He had a thick leather sports belt. "I'll slit it and slide the map inside," he said. "Then nobody will ever find it!"

Mr. Hollister drove his brother to the airport before returning to downtown Shoreham, where he operated *The Trading Post*. This was a combination hardware, toy, and sporting goods shop.

When the men had gone, the children spread the encyclopedias on the floor and Pam read aloud while Holly traced the glyphs of the months and days on two pieces of paper.

33

There were several pictures of ancient Mayas. "What large noses they have!" Ricky said.

"And see how their foreheads slope, too," was Holly's comment.

"Gee, I want to get to Itchin' Chicken as soon as I can!" Ricky declared.

This made Pete and Pam laugh.

"Not Itchin' Chicken," said Pam. "It's pronounced chee-CHEN eet-ZA. Look, it says here that means 'the mouth of the well of the Itzá tribe.'"

While Pam continued reading, Pete phoned headquarters. Officer Cal had not yet come on duty, but Pete learned that the suspect, Aguila, had landed in New York and slipped away before the police there could question him.

Pete reported the news to the others, then pondered over the tire tracks they had seen the night before. He snapped his fingers. "Pam! I bet I can find that car!"

His sister closed her book. "How will you do that?"

"If we can get to the Rent-A-Car Company at the airport, soon, I think it'll work. Come on, let's get our bikes, quick."

Pete and Pam told their mother where they were going, and ran for their bicycles. But before setting off, Pete bent down to look at a gadget attached to his front wheel. It measured how far the bicycle traveled. Pete set the numbers back to zero. As they rode Pete explained his plan to his sister. Half an hour later they pulled up alongside the airport building and set their bikes on the kickstands.

Before entering the building, Pete checked the mileage on the odometer. "Five and a quarter miles. Remember that, Pam."

They hastened to the car rental counter where a smiling young woman greeted them. "What can I do for you?" she asked.

"We'd like to check the mileage driven by a customer you had yesterday," Pete said.

"Goodness, you sound like detectives," the woman replied.

"To tell you the truth, we are," Pete said. "And this is very important. Could you help us, please?"

"I'll try to," came the reply. The pleasant woman reached into a file and pulled out a sheaf of reports. "We had ten customers yesterday afternoon," she said. "Eight of them reported back."

"Did any of them go a total of ten and a half miles?"

The woman checked her records as Pam grinned admiringly at her brother's clever sleuthing.

Suddenly an amazed look came over the woman's face. "How did you know that?" she asked. "Here's one that went exactly ten and a half miles."

"Who was the car rented by?" asked Pete.

"A man named Smith."

"It sure sounds like a phony name," Pam said. "I'll bet it was Aguila."

"There's one more favor I would like to ask,"

said Pete. "May we examine that particular car?"

"Really—now, you must be detectives!" the woman said smiling. Then she added, "The car has not been rented yet today. You'll find it at the side of the building near our sign. It's the newest sedan."

The youngsters thanked the woman and hurried to the Rent-A-Car stand. An attendant had just finished cleaning the sedan with a hand vacuum.

"We would like to examine this car," Pete said.

The attendant seemed amused and said, "What are you looking for?"

"We don't know yet," said Pam.

"Have you permission?"

"Yes," said Pete.

"Then go ahead. If you find anything in there, you're better than I am."

The two children opened the four doors of the car and searched the floor. Pam lifted the rubber mat. She could find nothing. "What kind of a clue are you looking for?" she whispered.

"I don't know," replied Pete. "But that Mr. Aguila might have dropped something."

The boy slid his hand between the back of the seat and the cushion. Nothing. "Do you mind if I lift this seat out?" Pete asked the attendant. The man shrugged. The children tugged hard and out came the seat.

"Look, Pam!" There lay three coins—a penny, a dime, and an odd silver coin with a serpent's head on it!

CHAPTER 4

THE CHICHÉN CHICKEN

PETE picked up the three coins and showed them to the attendant. "Look what we found!" he said.

"Are you lucky!" the man replied, helping the children to put the seat back in place. "That money wasn't there yesterday, because I cleaned under the seat!"

Pete and Pam thanked the man and hurried back inside to the Rent-A-Car counter.

"Did you find what you were looking for?" the woman asked.

Pete nodded and showed her the coins. "We found these under the front seat."

"How did you know they were there?"

"We didn't really," Pete replied, "it was only a hunch. You'd better take the eleven cents, but may we keep the coin with the serpent's head?"

"Well . . ." she said doubtfully.

"If anybody comes to claim it," added Pam quickly, "we'll give it back."

"In that case, all right," said the woman.

Pam wrote their name and address on a piece of paper and gave it to the clerk. Outside the terminal building, the two Hollisters paused beside their bikes to examine the coin. It was about the size of a fifty-cent piece and the serpent had a man's head.

"See how long the nose is," said Pam excitedly, "and the forehead slopes, too. It's a Mayan Indian —just like the pictures in the encyclopedia."

"This clinches it," said Pete. "Smith is Aguila. I bet he's on his way back to Yucatán to wait for Uncle Russ."

Pam gave a little shiver. "We'll have to keep our eyes open for him."

When Pete and Pam reached home they found Ricky, Holly, and Sue excitedly chattering over a phone call from Uncle Russ. "We're going in two days," Holly said, giving little Sue a hug to emphasize her words.

"Yes!" Ricky said. "On Uncle Russ's company airplane. It's coming to Shoreham for us on Sunday."

The next two days were filled with the excitement of preparing for their trip. The Hollisters had done this many times before, so everything went smoothly. As usual, Ann and Jeff Hunter, who lived down the street, volunteered to care for White Nose and her kittens. Dave Mead, a friend of Pete's, was only too happy to keep Zip during the Hollisters' absence. The family's pet burro, Domingo, had been loaned to their friend Farmer Johnson, who would be using him for several weeks.

"Mother," Pam said the day before they were to

leave, "may Holly and I go to the library to do some more reading about Yucatán?"

"Of course, dear, but be home in time for supper at six o'clock."

"Me too," piped little Sue.

"I'll take care of her," Pam said. She put Sue in the wire basket in front of her handlebars. Then she and Holly mounted their bikes and set off.

When they pedaled past Dave Mead's house, the girls saw Joey Brill coming toward them whacking a stick against the trees. As soon as he caught sight of the Hollisters, Joey let out a bloodcurdling yell and danced in front of the wheels, trying to jab his stick between the spokes.

"Watch out!" shouted Holly.

Pam swerved.

Crash! The bike hit a tree and Sue tumbled head over heels out of the basket and onto the grass. Her wailing brought Dave running out of the house and across his lawn.

"You can fight girls just great!" Dave shouted. "I'm going to punch you in the nose, Joey!"

"I'll help you," Holly yelled and leaped from her bike.

Joey dropped his stick and sprinted into the nearest back yard. "Ha-ha. You'll have to catch me first!" he taunted. With that he leaped a low hedge and the next moment gave a shrill cry.

When Dave and Holly caught up they found the bully floundering knee-deep in loose, mucky dirt.

Holly gasped. "Oh, oh! Mr. Ferguson's new rose bed! Are you going to get it!"

An angry shout sounded from the house and a stocky red-faced man burst out. He collared Joey, pulled him free of the mud, and gave him a whack on the pants.

When Joey ran off sniveling, Dave called after him: "Well, so long, Joey. Life is just a bed of roses!"

Grinning broadly, he and Holly returned to the bikes. They found Sue sitting in Pam's basket again, her tears dried.

"Thanks for your help, Dave," said Pam.

The boy chuckled. "No trouble. Did you hear about Joey's mutt?"

"I feel so sorry for that poor dog," Pam replied. "What happened?"

"When Joey tried to teach him to bite people, his mother gave the dog to some friends in Stony Point."

The girls rode off again. Pam said, "Dave's nice."

Holly grinned and gave her sister a sidelong glance.

By five-thirty the three girls were back from the library very much excited about what they had learned.

"Mommy!" cried Sue. "Pam found out more about that clue!"

"She means the coin we found," Pam said. "It's

"Oh, oh! Are you going to get it."

really a figure of Kukulcan, the serpent god of the Mayans."

"You remember. The one with the temple in Chichén Itzá," Holly put in.

"That's very interesting," their mother replied, and returned to the kitchen where she was preparing supper.

The girls followed her in, and Holly said, "Look, Mother!" Mrs. Hollister glanced down at her daughter, who was looking cross-eyed.

"Oh, Holly, you look so funny," her mother replied.

"No, I'm beautiful!"

When Pam heard this she hastened to tell her mother that the ancient Mayans thought that cross eyes were a sign of beauty.

"But I'm sure it isn't that way today," Mrs. Hollister said, smiling.

When little Sue began to look cross-eyed too, her mother declared: "Now girls, stop that! You're making me nervous. I might burn the lamb chops!"

The two younger sisters giggled, then raced into the living room to show the boys what beautiful maidens looked like.

"Oh, that's nothing," Ricky said. He crossed his eyes, put his thumbs in his ears, and wriggled his fingers, and the girls burst out laughing.

"Come, now, wash for supper," Mrs. Hollister said, and her youngsters scampered off.

Early the next morning the Hollisters packed their

belongings into the station wagon. Sue kissed Mathilda good-by before climbing into the car, and Mr. Hollister drove to the airport. Pete wore his wide leather belt with Uncle Russ's map tucked safely in it. By the time they arrived, a small private jet was waiting for them.

The pilot, a tall, stout, jolly man wearing a business suit, introduced himself as Tom Mulvey.

"Come on," he said, leading them to the aircraft. "We'll have you in the middle of the Yucatán jungle in no time at all."

Several hours later, as the children gazed out of the plane window, they saw a huge city spread out below them.

"That's New Orleans," the pilot said. "Now we're crossing the Gulf of Mexico. In a little over an hour we should land in Mérida—Yucatán's capital."

Finally the children felt a funny sensation in their ears, as the plane began to descend.

"Yikes, what a small city!" Ricky said, looking at the town coming up under their left wing.

"Those are the jungles over there to your right," the pilot said.

As the plane winged lower, the travelers saw a dense forest of trees, about thirty feet high.

"Where are the Indians?" Ricky questioned.

"They're in there all right. You'll see plenty of them," Mrs. Hollister said.

Finally the wheels touched down on the runway

and the jet roared to a stop. Then it taxied up before a low, white building.

"Crickets!" Pete said. "Is this the terminal?"

"That's right," the pilot replied, as he helped the family down the steps to the ground. "It's not even as big as Shoreham's!"

Mrs. Hollister led her children through the customs, where a man in a uniform checked their identification. "Enjoy yourself in Mexico," he said.

All at once Holly shrieked, "Teddy, Jean, Aunt Marge!"

Their cousins stood smiling at the exit, and the children ran to greet them. "Hurray! We're going on an adventure!" Ricky shouted.

Aunt Marge was slender, dark-haired and pretty, with a humorous twinkle in her eyes. Her daughter Jean, who was nine, had straight chestnut hair and dimples, which now stood out prettily.

Teddy looked something like his cousin Pete. A year younger, he had black hair, gray eyes and seemed always on the move.

The two mothers embraced and talked excitedly about their trip.

"Russ will be here in a few days," said Aunt Marge, who was carrying a large knitting bag. "Oh, there's so much to see in Chichén!"

When the porter had taken their luggage, the Hollister cousins and the two women walked outside toward an old station wagon.

A slim man wearing blue trousers and an open

gray shirt, greeted the travelers cordially. His face was tanned and wrinkled beneath a floppy white hat, and his long broad nose hinted of Mayan Indian ancestry.

"Balám is an old friend of Skeets's," Aunt Marge said, "and he'll take good care of us."

Giggling and laughing, the children scrambled into the car, while Balám lifted their baggage to a rack atop the station wagon and tied it securely.

"Are we going into Mérida?" asked Pete.

"No. Directly to Chichén," said Balám with a smile.

The narrow black-top road, flanked by woods on either side, led eastward over the rolling country.

How different everything looked from Shoreham and the United States! And how much hotter it was!

"You'll be comfortable at the *hacienda* in Chichén Itzá," Aunt Marge said. "It's only about a two-hour ride from here."

The car passed a little group of huts beside the road, and shy brown children playing in front ducked into the doorways.

"Are they Indians?" Pam asked the driver.

"Yes. Mayans."

"Marge," put in Mrs. Hollister, "I think you should know what happened in Shoreham just before we left." Quickly she and her children told the story of the briefcase.

Aunt Marge looked worried. "I'm afraid this trip

is going to be dangerous. Maybe you should not have come."

Pete grinned. "Nonsense! We Hollisters have to stick together."

Just then a pickup truck, piled high with crates, sped in their direction.

"Look," said Holly, "a load of chickens."

At that moment a skinny brown dog started to cross the road. The truck swerved toward the Hollisters' car.

"Look out!" cried Ricky, but it was too late! With a fearful scraping noise, the vehicles sideswiped!

CHAPTER 5

HOLEE-STARE

As THE CHICKEN TRUCK rattled past, one of the crates fell from the top and landed with a thud on the Hollisters' car. Then it bounced off to the side of the road, broke open, and four chickens ran squawking into the jungle.

Balám stopped the car quickly and the Hollisters got out to look at the damage. The truck driver increased his speed and soon was out of sight.

Balám gazed sadly at the side of the station wagon. It was gouged and scraped.

"That driver shouldn't have left the scene of an accident," Mrs. Hollister said.

"Could you identify the truck, Balám?" Pete asked. The driver shrugged and gestured with his hands. "He came so fast. It was a pickup truck, green and dusty, that's all I can say."

Holly and Ricky, meanwhile, discovered the crate, then caught sight of one of the chickens bobbing in a thicket at the jungle's edge.

"Come on, Holly, let's get him!" They tiptoed off at first, then dashed into the brush.

"Look!" Ricky said. "There's four of them!" Three of the chickens seemed lively enough as they

47

ran deeper into the jungle, but the fourth one limped.

Holly easily caught her, and returned to the road carrying the fowl under one arm.

"The three others got away," Ricky said.

"Goodness!" Aunt Marge exclaimed. "What are you going to do with the chicken?"

"Keep him, of course," said Holly.

"Well," her mother said, "let's carry the bird as far as Chichén Itzá. Perhaps we can give it to one of the natives there."

Holly pouted a little. "I caught it and it's mine," she said.

Jean giggled. "Holly finds pets wherever she goes! What are you going to call your chicken?"

"Oh, Sue's good at naming things," Pam spoke up, as they returned to the car.

They all looked at the little dark-haired girl, who climbed into her seat, rolled her eyes and thought very hard.

"I think her name should be Tan-Tan," she said.

"That's an odd one," Aunt Marge remarked, as Balám got behind the wheel.

"That's the name of this country, isn't it?" asked Sue, and they all laughed.

Suddenly a shout came from Pete, who had walked a few yards down the road. He raced back to the car, waving what appeared to be a tennis ball. "Hey, I found something, and I'll bet it's ancient."

Even the chicken stretched her neck to look at

Pete's find. It was a ball carved of stone. One side was rough, as if it had broken off from something else.

Balám took the ball in his hand, turning it over and over as he examined it closely. Finally he said, "This is an earplug from a rain god!"

"Yikes!" Ricky said. "What does that mean?"

Patiently Balám told them that the ball had been an ear decoration on a carved stone idol.

"But how did it get out here?" asked Pam.

The guide shook his head. There were no temple pyramids in the vicinity.

"Then maybe it fell off that chicken truck," Pam suggested.

"What would it be doing on a chicken truck?" asked Teddy.

"Anyhow," Aunt Marge said, "it must be returned to the Mexican authorities."

Balám agreed, explaining that many of the ancient objects found around the pyramids were being taken out of the country illegally. "Anything you find must be given back," he went on, "so that it can be used when the pyramids are reconstructed."

As Balám drove on again, Pete studied the stone ball while the others talked about Chichén Itzá.

"It was founded about A.D. four hundred," said Aunt Marge, "but there were Mayans around before then."

"A funny thing," Teddy put in. "Chichén was occupied for about two hundred years, then abandoned until the year one thousand. The Itzá tribe came back and rebuilt the city."

"Why all the pyramids?" Pete asked.

Balám spoke up. He said that after the Mayan people had planted their corn and harvested the crop, the leaders kept everyone busy by building temples.

Aunt Marge said, "If you stand on a high place, you can see bumps all over the forest. Those are the unexcavated pyramids overgrown with trees and vines."

"One is the Temple of the Laughing Idol," Ricky said importantly.

"That's deep in the jungle," Balám remarked. "I don't know if we can ever find it!"

"But we have a m—" Pete bit his tongue. Even among friends, he meant to keep silent about the secret map he carried in his belt.

Pam quickly changed the subject to the arrival of the Spanish in Yucatán. Jean told her that the Mayans were conquered in the year 1697 by an expedition under the command of Martín D. Urzia.

Talking about Mexico made the time go fast and soon the car pulled up at the side of the road. There amid flowering bushes stood a neat hacienda.

"Here's your hotel," Balám said and stepped out. He began to remove the luggage.

"Do you live here too?" Pam asked her cousins.

"No, we're in the annex, down the road a bit."

But all the youngsters helped carry the luggage

into the sunny courtyard and put it down beside a bubbling fountain.

"We live in a wilder place than this," Teddy whispered. "As soon as you're unpacked, come on over! It's down the road and through the gate."

"Sure, see you later," Pete replied, and Teddy and Jean went off with their mother.

The hotel manager led the Hollisters across the court into the two large, cool rooms they were to occupy. He raised his eyebrows when he saw the chicken under Holly's arm. "I'm afraid we don't allow fowl in here," he said politely.

"Tan-Tan has a hurt leg," little Sue protested.

"Then I know a good place for her," the manager said.

Taking Sue by the hand, the man led her and Holly across a patio, and down a flight of stone steps to a swimming pool, then around the back of the hacienda, where they found a small pen under a bushy tree.

"Tan-Tan can stay here," the man said, smiling. "We used to keep a dove in the cage, but it's gone now."

Sue was satisfied. She lifted the top of the pen, which was made of narrow strips of wood, and Holly put the chicken inside. "We'll get some food for you soon," she said, and the sisters returned to their family.

As soon as Pete and Pam had unpacked, they

told their mother they were going to visit Teddy and Jean.

They went across the road, walked down several hundred yards and found a gate leading into a little settlement. Several native thatched-roof houses lined the road, and next to these stood four small frame dwellings. From the end one, Teddy and Jean hastened out to meet their cousins.

"Crickets, this is keen!" Pete said, glancing around.

"And you should see the church we have here," said Jean. She led them along a path past a tall dead tree in which several dozen huge black birds roosted.

"Those are vultures," Teddy said. "Aren't they weird?"

A few of the huge birds spread their black wings and flew off. Following the trail through high bushes, the children saw only two goats nibbling at the leaves alongside it. Then the church came into view. It was an old Spanish type with three iron bells hanging in arches on the roof. From the bell on the right side, a rope hung nearly to the ground.

"They sound wonderful," said Jean. "We hear them in the morning."

"And late at night too, sometimes," Teddy added. "A few of the natives say the bells are haunted."

"Impossible," Pete said, laughing.

"Then how do you explain the midnight ringing," Teddy persisted.

"Maybe somebody's playing a joke," Pam said.

Jean shook her head. "People are very quiet here. I don't think anybody would do such a thing."

The children walked around the old church, which stood at the edge of the jungle. Then they stepped into the dim, cool interior and searched for a clue to the ghostly ringing. Finding nothing, they hurried back to the cabins where Aunt Marge met them at the door. "If you're ready," she said, "we can all go to lunch, and then visit the pyramid of Kukulcan."

The whole family sat down at a long table in the hacienda and enjoyed a lunch of fresh fruit salad and tall glasses of cool milk.

Then, with Teddy and Jean in the lead, they trooped along the road, and soon entered the great plaza of the Temple of Kukulcan.

"Oh, it's fantastic!" declared Pam.

Before them towered a pyramid, with steep stairways in the center of each of the four sides leading to the temple on the top platform.

"Let's climb it right now," Pete said.

"No, wait. I want to show you a better place," Ted said.

"Yes—the ball court!" Jean exclaimed. "Come on!"

Leaving the two mothers gazing at the pyramid, the children hastened after Teddy and Jean until they came to a long, grassy stretch flanked at either side by high walls.

"This is where the Mayans played ball," said Teddy.

"Where are the bases?" asked Ricky.

His cousin laughed. "There weren't any bases. See up there?" He pointed to a huge stone ring embedded in one of the walls.

"They had to knock the ball through that hole just once to win the game."

"Crickets," Pete said. "It wouldn't be hard to throw a ball through there."

"But they couldn't throw it," Jean said. "They had to hit the ball with their elbows, knees, or body, but they couldn't throw it."

"Yikes! That would be hard," Ricky admitted.

"But the worst thing of all," Teddy continued, "is what happened to the losing captain."

"What?" asked Holly.

"He lost his head!" said Teddy.

"You're fooling!" said Ricky.

"Teddy's right," Jean said. "The loser would have his head cut off by the winning captain."

"Come over here, I'll show you a picture of how they did it." Teddy beckoned.

The children walked toward a long carved stone at one side of the court. The figures of players with plumed headdresses were intertwined with snake designs, but Jean carefully pointed out the winning captain and his victim.

"Ugh!" Holly said.

"There's something else peculiar about this

"Where are the bases?" asked Ricky.

court," Teddy went on. "You can hear a whisper from one end to the other."

The youngsters trooped to the far end of the court, where they stopped. Turning back, they saw two men walking slowly to the opposite side, talking earnestly.

"Now," Teddy said, "Ricky, you run down where those men are and whisper. I'll bet we can hear you, and we'll whisper back."

But before the boy could move, the voices of the two men reached the children. "See what I mean?" Teddy asked.

They listened quietly to the babble of Spanish, but suddenly a startled look came over their faces as the words "Holee stare" drifted to their ears. "Holee stare," Pete said. "Crickets, I bet that's Hollister! They're talking about us!"

CHAPTER 6

THE MYSTERY MEN

"HOLEE-STARE!" Pete said. "That's Hollister with a Spanish accent."

"Something funny's going on," Ricky said, shielding his eyes from the sun in order to get a better look at the two men.

The odd acoustics of the ball court carried the boys' words to the other end, and the men turned quickly. Seeing the children, they hurried behind the wall of the ancient court. The Hollisters raced after them, but they had disappeared.

Just then Balám walked up to the visitors, a big smile on his face. Ricky told him they had heard the story of the ancient ball game, and Balám replied: "Oh, you mean pok-a-tok." He nodded his head and added, "Do you have witch stories in your country?"

"Witches? Oh, yes," Holly replied. "Especially at Halloween."

"How would you like to hear a story about a Mayan witch?"

"We'd love it," Pam said. She sat on the grass cross-legged and looked around for Sue.

"I think she went back to our mothers," said Jean.

Pete chuckled. "Probably got scared by that ball court story."

The youngsters listened eagerly as Balám told them about La Bruja, the ancient witch of Cabah. This sorceress had a son born from an iguana egg. When it cracked open, out stepped a dwarf with an iguana's spine.

"You mean one of those little lizards that we once saw in Puerto Rico?" Ricky interrupted.

Balám said that the ones in Yucatán were large, and with his hands indicated a creature of more than two feet long.

"This little dwarf was very smart," Balám continued, "and in a few years he wanted to be the king. But first he had to pass a test."

"What was it?" asked Holly.

"Anyone who wanted to be a king had to have a coconut cracked on his head. So the witch made a copper cap for her little son. When the coconut was cracked on his head, it didn't hurt him. But the ruling monarch's head was split and he died, so the dwarf became king."

"Yikes! Was that for real?" Ricky asked, his eyes round with excitement.

"Who knows," said Balám, shrugging. "There is a statue of the sorceress in a little grotto in the jungle of Cabah."

"May we see it sometime?" asked Jean.

"I think so. Maybe when we go to Uxmal." Balám pronounced it Oosh-mal.

When Jean asked about this, Balám told her that the X had a *sh* sound in the Mayan language.

At that moment, Mrs. Hollister and Aunt Marge appeared from around the wall of the ball court. They stopped for a moment and a look of concern came over their faces. "Where's Sue?" Mrs. Hollister cried, hurrying toward the children.

Pam jumped up, startled. "I thought she went to find you, Mother."

"We haven't seen her," Aunt Marge replied.

The children quickly looked all around the ball court, but could not find the little girl.

"Maybe she went to the cenote," said Jean in a frightened voice.

"Is it near here?" Mrs. Hollister asked.

"Oh, yes," Aunt Marge replied, pointing. "It's over this way. Come, hurry!"

They started down a dusty path which led through heavy thickets. Several sightseers were coming slowly toward them.

"Did you pass a little girl walking alone?" Pam asked the first woman.

"Yes, we did. About five years old with black hair?"

"That's Sue," declared Holly. "Our sister is lost!"

"I wish I had known that. I would have brought her back. When I passed her, she was nearly to the cenote."

Now all the Hollisters ran, everybody with the same thought in mind. If little Sue should get too close to the edge, she might fall into the deep well!

Finally the thicket gave way to a great open space and Pete, in the lead, caught sight of Sue. She was standing at the lip of the cenote, leaning down and looking into the water.

The boy slackened his pace so as not to frighten her, then quickly grabbed one of her chubby wrists, and pulled her back from the edge. "Sue, you shouldn't wander off like that!" he said, as the others reached them.

Mrs. Hollister clutched the little girl in a warm embrace.

"Don't worry, I wouldn't fall in like the Tan-Tan maidens," declared Sue.

As Balám caught up to them, the family stood back to marvel at the huge cenote. It was more or less circular and, the guide said, sixty-five yards in diameter. He explained that the porous lime-stone, which extended over all Yucatán, had caved in here, revealing part of the great table of water which underlay the area.

"There are no rivers in Yucatán," Balám said. "All the water lies under the ground."

Pam gazed at the vertical sides. "It looks like a long way down!"

Balám nodded. "It is sixty feet down to the water level."

"How deep is the water?" Ricky asked.

"About forty feet," the man replied, "and at the bottom is a ten-foot layer of mud."

"Sue, you shouldn't wander off!"

The guide explained that in recent weeks an expedition from an American university had been dredging up the mud to look for precious relics from the past.

"Did they find any?" asked Ricky.

"A few things, like rings and jewels and brooches which had been thrown into the well as sacrifices."

As they left the cenote, Pam told the women and Balám about the two mysterious men.

"Are you sure they mentioned our name?" Aunt Marge asked.

"Quite sure," the girl replied. "I hope we see them again."

"Yes, then we can ask them about it," Mrs. Hollister said.

Ricky, meanwhile, had dashed on ahead, kicking up dust along the trail.

"Boy," he thought, "I'd like to go fishing in that well!" This idea vanished when the giant pyramid came into view.

"And now," Balám said, "let's climb to the top of Kukulcan. The steps are too tall for Sue, but I'll carry her on my back."

At the foot of the huge pyramid, the travelers looked to the top. Its height and grandness made it the most imposing monument in all of Chichén Itzá. Balám said the pyramid was twenty-five yards high, with nine terraces and a square base. Each of its sides was sixty yards long.

They started to mount the huge steps and Aunt

Marge told the children that there were ninety-one steps on each of the four stairways, making a total of three hundred and sixty-four steps.

"And that, plus the upper platform, which is one step more, makes three hundred and sixty-five," she said, "the number of days in our year."

"It's kind of spooky, isn't it," said Ricky. "They must have known a lot about the solar system."

Sue was having more fun than anybody. She giggled and clung tightly to the guide, her chubby arms hugging his neck as they worked their way upward. Finally they reached the top and gazed out over the jungle.

"The forest looks as if it had a crew cut," Pete said with a chuckle. The trees, stretching into the distance, were all about thirty feet high.

Suddenly Pam saw two men walking near the base of the temple. She grabbed Pete's arm, and exclaimed, "Look! They're the ones who were talking about us!"

"You're right!" Pete replied. "Let's catch them!" He and Teddy started down the opposite face of the pyramid to approach the men from the back. Balám, meanwhile, descended with Pam and Jean, while the two women followed with the younger children.

Pete and Teddy leaped like jaguars from step to step until they reached the bottom of the pyramid. They quickly spotted the men, and hurried up behind them.

"Wait!" Pete called out. They turned about, looking surprised. One of them was short and stout and had a black mustache. The other was slightly taller with a thin, wrinkled face, which made him look as if he were sucking in his cheeks.

"Ah!" said the mustached man. "You are speaking to me?"

"Yes, I am," Pete replied, and introduced himself and his cousin. "We heard you mention our name at the ball court. Are you looking for us?"

The man's black eyebrows arched like a slowly pulled bow. He spoke with a heavy Spanish accent.

"I am Señor Punto," he said and, with a small bow to his companion, added, "This is Señor Vargas, a friend I have not seen in years."

"But why did you mention our name?" came the voice of Pam, as she hastened up with the others from the opposite side.

Señor Punto wheeled about. At first he seemed agitated, but then regained his composure.

"I am looking for a man named Russell Holeestare."

"That's my father," said Teddy. "What do you want of him?"

Punto rubbed his hands together and said, "There is a Señor Skeets Packer in the States. He has written to me to be on the lookout for Señor Holeestare."

CHAPTER 7

A MIDNIGHT PROWLER

AUNT MARGE spoke up. "Why do you wish to see my husband?"

"To help him find the lost temple," Punto replied quickly.

"When he arrives, we'll tell him," Aunt Marge went on. "Where are you staying, Señor Punto?"

"I am camping," the man said, "but I will be nearby. You will find me easy."

When the two men were out of earshot, Pam said, "I don't trust that Señor Punto. Did you see how nervous he was? I'll bet he wasn't telling the truth."

"Our jungle trip was supposed to be so secret," said Teddy. "How does Punto know about it?"

All the Hollisters agreed there was something mysterious going on, especially since Balám said that he had never seen Señor Punto or his friend before, nor had he heard of them.

"That Vargas gives me the creeps," said Ricky.

"Maybe these two are connected with Aguila," said Pam.

"Could be," Pete agreed.

The Shoreham Hollisters returned to the little

hotel, promising to meet their cousins for supper in half an hour.

With hands and faces washed, the beaming cousins joined their mothers at the table. Each was handed a menu by a pretty Mayan waitress wearing a long white dress. For a while all sat quietly, studying the words which were written both in English and Spanish.

"I would like to have *sopa de tomate*," Pam said, her eyes dancing with delight.

"Yikes, that's only tomato soup!" exclaimed Ricky.

"I'll have some of that soap too," said Pete with a wink.

When Jean ordered *camarones ala mexicana*, which meant shrimp, Mexican style, Holly said, "I'll have some cameras too!"

The waitress glided back and forth, hardly making a sound as she served the Hollisters with speed and grace.

"I wonder what they call those dresses?" said Ricky.

"Why would a boy want to know that?" Holly teased.

"'Cause they look like nighties!" Ricky blurted.

"All right then, we'll find out," his mother said. She beckoned to the hostess, who told them that the dresses were *huipils*, pronounced ee-peels. "This is the costume for Mayan women," she said. "The square yokes at the neck are hand embroidered in many colors."

"Are you satisfied, Ricky?" asked Pam.

"Ee-peel, schmee-peel," said Ricky. "They still look like nighties."

Near the end of the meal, both Ricky and Holly quietly put pieces of bread in their pockets; and when the chairs were pushed back, Holly took her half-full glass of water and hastened to Tan-Tan's pen. The girl put the bread and water in with the clucking chicken and said, "There! Now you have plenty to eat and drink."

Just then Ricky appeared around the corner.

"I saw you take some bread, too," Holly said. "Are you going to feed Tan-Tan?"

"Nope. I'm looking for string. Did you see any around?"

"No, but Aunt Marge has a big ball of yarn in her knitting bag."

Ricky hastened around the hacienda and caught up with his aunt, who was strolling toward the annex with Mrs. Hollister.

"Can I have a piece of your knitting yarn?" he asked.

"Certainly," she replied. "The bag is next to my chair on the porch."

Ricky ran ahead, and helped himself to the whole ball of yarn. Then he raced back past the hotel, alongside the pyramid and down the trail toward the cenote.

Arriving at the edge of the well, Ricky tied a safety pin to one end of the yarn. After rolling a small piece of bread into a ball, he put it on the hook, which he lowered over the side of the cenote. More and more yarn was let out, and finally Ricky felt the hook reach the water.

"I bet there's a giant fish down there," the boy said to himself, clinging tightly to the other end of the yarn. He waited and waited, but nothing bit his hook.

"Maybe I'm at the wrong spot," he thought, and started to walk around the cenote, taking care to stay a foot or so from the lip.

All at once there was a light tug on the line! Ricky yelled, "I've got something!" He pulled the yarn up hand over hand. But there was no fish at the end! Instead the hook held a small ring!

Several tourists who had heard Ricky cry out came over to see what he had found.

"That must be very valuable," one woman said. Her husband examined the ring too. "It looks like copper," he said. "Must have been thrown into the well by the ancient Mayans."

Ricky felt very proud as he held the tangled yarn in one hand, and the ring in the other. He began to trot toward the hacienda. Halfway down the path, he met Señor Punto.

"What have you got there?" the man asked in a kindly tone.

"A real old ring from ancient days!" Ricky said.

"What have you got there?"

Señor Punto walked over, took the relic in his hands, and examined it carefully.

"This is a real treasure," he said. "If I were you, I wouldn't report it to the government."

"Oh, but I must," Ricky said. "It isn't right not to."

Punto gave the boy a crooked smile, passed the ring back to him, and sauntered off.

When word of Ricky's discovery circulated around the hacienda, many people came to look at the ring.

"It must have been stirred up by the university searchers," Balám said.

The hotel manager supplied a little copper cleaner and Pam worked on the ring until it glowed beautifully.

"The authorities have been notified," the manager said. "They will probably come for the ring in the morning."

"They can take the earplug at the same time," said Pete.

As it grew dark, Ricky and Holly begged to spend the night with Teddy and Jean in the annex.

"Aren't you afraid of the haunted bell?" Pam teased the redhead.

"'Course not," he replied, grinning. "There aren't any spooks in Yucatán."

Their cousins were glad to have company. Ricky would sleep with Teddy, and Holly with Jean.

After both mothers had given their permission,

the youngsters gathered up their pajamas and tooth-brushes. Ricky thrust the ring into his pocket and Holly raced out to say good night to Tan-Tan.

As the children walked down the road, they could see the old dead tree looming up grotesquely into the sky. Its branches were black with roosting vultures. Behind it the silhouette of the church stood out dimly in the gathering darkness.

After Ricky had skinned into his pajamas, he and Teddy talked for a while before going to sleep. In the middle of the night both boys awoke suddenly. A gentle *ding-dong* was coming through the darkness.

"Oh-oh," said Ricky. "The ghost is ringing the church bell."

"I don't believe that," Teddy said. "Let's go see who's doing it. But don't turn on the light. We don't want to wake the others."

The boys quickly got into their clothes and tiptoed from the house. As they groped along the path leading to the church, a dark figure suddenly loomed up before them!

The cousins froze with fright, unable to scream, as a man clapped a hand over their mouths.

"Ugh! Umpf!" The startled boys struggled to free themselves, and Teddy tore loose from the grip. He lashed out, but hit empty air, as the man wrestled with Ricky.

Then the attacker let go and melted into the darkness.

CHAPTER 8

YO TAM HAI

THE TWO BOYS stood shaking in the darkness. All was quiet, save for the gentle ringing of the bell.

Suddenly Ricky reached into his pocket and exclaimed, "My ring—it's gone! That man stole it!"

"I'll bet he meant to rob us while we slept," said Teddy. "And then when we came out—zowie!"

Realizing that they could not find the thief in the darkness, the boys turned their attention to the bell again.

"I bet it's some kind of a signal," Teddy declared. "Come on, Ricky, let's find out!"

The younger boy clenched his chattering teeth and followed his cousin. Now the outline of the church could be seen, and the boys looked first to the swinging bell, then to the rope dangling near the ground.

Suddenly Ricky burst out laughing. "Look!" he sputtered. "A goat!"

They approached closer to see the small animal nibbling on the end of the rope and ringing the bell.

"Get away from there!" Teddy said. "You'll wake up the whole neighborhood."

He gave the goat a slap on the flank, and it scooted off into the darkness.

The boys returned to the annex and went back to sleep. They did not report their adventures until the following morning. Everybody was aghast over the bold theft.

Shortly after breakfast a policeman arrived to pick up the ring and the boys told their experience.

"Too bad the ring was stolen," the officer said in halting English. "Many of our treasures are being lost to thieves."

Then Pete gave the policeman the earplug he had found. The man quickly confirmed that it was from a rain god. "Probably stolen near Uxmal."

Pam explained about the chicken truck and said that she thought the ornament had fallen off it.

The policeman shrugged. "I doubt it. Our natives don't steal from pyramids."

Shortly after the officer had left, the hotel manager hurried over to Aunt Marge with a paper in his hand.

"A telegram for you, Mrs. Hollister," he said. "It was phoned from Mérida."

Aunt Marge read the message, and exclaimed, "Oh, no!"

"What happened, is anything wrong?" Jean asked.

"Nothing, except that Daddy isn't coming right away," her mother said. The telegram advised the Hollisters to move on to the Hacienda Copal near

Uxmal. "This is closer to where we will search for the Laughing Idol Temple," Aunt Marge said, and added, "Daddy will join us there as soon as he can."

Before lunchtime the Hollisters packed their suitcases, which were then stowed aboard Balám's station wagon. Even Tan-Tan, the chicken, complaining a little, had her pen lashed securely to the top of the car. After eating, the travelers said good-by to the people in the hacienda, and drove off along the road leading deeper into the jungle of Yucatán.

"I hope that Señor Punto and his friend don't see us leave," Pam said. "They might follow and cause trouble." But the mysterious men were not among the sightseers they passed on the way.

The ride to Hacienda Copal was pleasant, a light breeze cooling the hot faces of the youngsters, who were not used to temperatures which hovered about a hundred degrees. As they neared the place, Balám said that *copal* was a Mayan word for incense.

"It must be a sweet place to stay," quipped Teddy and Pete poked his cousin in the ribs.

"Say, this *is* a honey of a place!" he exclaimed as they drove into Hacienda Copal.

Before them, partly concealed among lush green palm trees, was a small, two-story hotel with twin wings, forming half a quadrangle.

In the middle of the grounds, looking like a beautiful green turquoise, was a swimming pool, with a stream of water gurgling in at one end.

"It's heavenly!" said Pam. As soon as the car had stopped, she ran down to the side of the pool, followed by Jean and Holly.

"What is that little hut, Pam?" asked Jean. On a rise of ground, twenty paces from the pool, was a shelter made of bamboo poles with a thatched roof. Through the open door the girls could see several people sitting on low stools.

"They're making something," said Holly and hastened over.

"It's an art and crafts shop!" Pam exclaimed.

A woman in her *huipil* and a man wearing an open shirt and white, rolled-up trousers were painting bright red, green, and blue colors on small figurines. They smiled at the children, who looked on shyly. Then Pam noticed that the ground behind the shop dipped sharply and a quarter of a mile distant lay a little native village.

"What's that?" Pam asked the man, hoping that he could speak English.

He smiled, put down his brush and looked up at the girl. "That is where most of the people live who work at the hacienda."

"May we go down there?" asked Holly.

Now the woman smiled and nodded. "We're Mr. and Mrs. Rico, and our house is the first one. See it?" she pointed. "When you get there ask for Tomás and Yotam."

"Your children?" asked Pam.

"Yes," the man replied. "They'll show you

around." The three girls descended a long cement stairway and found themselves at a narrow path leading to the settlement. Beside the huts they could see little gardens and in them were goats, dogs, and turkeys whose feathers glistened in the sunlight.

When they came to the house indicated by the craftsman's wife, Pam stepped forward and put her head into the open doorway. Inside, a girl, about six, was playing with a doll, and a boy of Pam's age was swinging in a hammock strung between two posts.

"Hello," said Pam. The boy stopped swinging and the little girl moved toward her brother.

"Are you Tomás and Yotam Rico?" Jean asked.

Their faces lighted. "Sí. I am Tomás," the boy said. "It is fine English I speak."

"Yes, you do well," agreed Pam. "And does Yotam speak English too?" The girl looked up, her big brown eyes very serious.

"A lee-tle," she said.

Now Holly spoke up. "Yotam is a funny name."

At this Tomás laughed. "It is made up," he said. "Because my sister always said, 'yo tam hai,' which means, 'Me too.' So we call her Yotam."

Glancing around the hut, the Hollister girls saw colorful blankets hung on poles at the side. A table and benches were set against one wall, and there was a wooden cupboard for dishes, pots, and pans.

"Are you Tomás and Yotam Rico?"

Outside, near the door, stood an open fireplace which contained charred wood and a few live coals.

"Would you show us around the village?" Jean asked Tomás. He nodded, smiling.

"*Yo tam hai,*" said Yotam, and the children walked through the little lanes of the village. Women, wearing *huipils,* waved from the doorways, and one beckoned to them. She offered them a piece of bread with honey.

"We have nice bees in Yucatán," said Tomás. "They don't sting you."

"I'm glad to hear that," said Holly, who hated to have bees buzzing around her head.

The children thanked the woman, and ate their bread and honey. "Umm," said Holly, happily sucking at the end of her fingers.

Back in the hut, Pam looked curiously at the hammock. It was made out of material like fish netting.

"I don't see any beds," she said.

"We sleep in hammocks," the boy replied. "Would you like to try mine?"

"I don't know—"

"Don't be afraid. You won't fall down."

With the other girls watching, Pam wriggled her way into the hammock and began to rock back and forth.

"Not bad at all," she said. "In fact, it's great!"

Holly got up and gave her sister a good push.

The hammock swayed to and fro, and Pam let out a little cry.

Then Holly impishly gave her another strong push, and—*flip!*

Spun inside the hammock, Pam was caught like a fish!

CHAPTER 9

THE OLD RAILROAD

"Help, get me out of here!" Pam cried.

But the more she wriggled, the tighter she became entangled in the net hammock. Holly was helpless with giggles, but Jean said, "Lie still, Pam, we'll get you out!"

She and Tomás put their fingers into the cords of the hammock and carefully turned it over.

"Now she's unzippered!" gasped Holly, as her sister climbed free. "I'm sorry, Pam," Holly added, trying not to laugh. "But it was so funny."

"Not to me," said her sister, but she grinned as she tidied her hair.

Then she told Tomás about her brothers and cousin Teddy. "Why don't you come up to the hacienda with us?" she asked. "I know the boys would love to go exploring with you."

But Tomás suddenly looked mysterious, and said he had something else to do. Without another word he raced out the door.

"Where's he going?" asked Holly, surprised.

Yotam pointed out the window and they saw the boy dash into the jungle behind the house.

"Is he mad at us?" Jean asked Yotam.

The little girl looked up sadly and shook her head. "No. But I think my brother is bewitched."

"Bewitched!" Pam declared. "What makes you think that, Yotam?"

The girl said that her brother ran off into the jungle every day, and would not tell where he went or what he did.

"I'd follow him sometime," Holly said. "He's probably got a big secret in the forest and doesn't want to tell you about it."

"But I cannot go into jungle," Yotam said haltingly, "because Tomás says that a witch lives in there." Her eyes filled with tears. "I am afraid that sometime he will not come back."

"Well," Pam said, "we're detectives and we'll find out where your brother goes. Then you won't have to worry anymore."

"The witch will not hurt you?" asked Yotam timidly.

Pam smiled and patted the little girl on the head. "We can take care of witches," she said.

"Yes, but first we'd better go back and unpack our clothes," declared Jean. They said good-by to the little Mayan girl, then walked back to the hacienda.

After unpacking, the girls looked about for their brothers, but they were nowhere in sight. In the lobby they met their mothers talking to a tall friendly man with gray sideburns and mustache. He was introduced as Mr. Cortez, the hotel manager.

81

"Excuse me, Mother," said Pam, "but do you know where the boys went?"

"Oh, the boys are off exploring," she replied.

At that very moment, Pete, Teddy, and Ricky had pushed a hundred feet into the jungle beside the road.

"Yikes! We'd better not get lost," Ricky said.

"Hey, look! Railroad tracks!" Pete shouted suddenly. The others ran over to him, and gazed on the ground. Nearly concealed by the weeds and thickets, were two steel tracks of a narrow-gauge railroad.

"Let's follow these, then we can't get lost," Teddy said.

The cousins pushed through the jungle slowly. Sometimes the tracks were entirely covered by green vegetation, and the boys had to tear it aside to find them.

"This old thing must lead to *someplace!*" Ricky said, after they had gone about a mile.

"Maybe it goes to a seaport," said Teddy and added, "Pete, I think we've come far enough. We'd better get back to the hacienda and find out just where the railroad went to."

His words were interrupted by a queer bird call, coming from the forest ahead of them. It sounded like a crow, but two long caws were followed by two short ones.

"Come on, let's go back," Ricky whispered, tugging at Pete's hand.

As they turned, Teddy saw a flash in the green ahead of them. He strained to see what it was and his eyes popped open. The light was made by the sun glancing off the tip of a spear!

"Down!" Teddy gasped, and the boys flattened into the brush.

Suddenly out of the trees ran four warriors, wearing the garb of ancient Mayans. Their feathered headdresses waved as they dashed after a fifth, with their weapons raised as if to spear him!

"Crickets!" Pete whispered. "We've run into a war!"

Suddenly someone yelled "Cut!" and the warriors stopped in their tracks.

"They're making movies!" Pete blurted out. The boys rose slowly to their feet and peered through the jungle at the warriors who were dragging their spears back along a trail.

But they hardly recovered from one fright when a bloodthirsty cry sounded behind them. With mouths agape, the boys wheeled to see another painted warrior glowering, his face contorted in anger.

"Who—who are you?" Pete barely got the words out of his parched throat.

"I am Alexis Regente!" the man said. "And you are trespassing on our property. Get out!"

"Are you an—an actor?" Pete asked, slowly backing away.

"An actor, he asks me! I am the leading man!"

"Crickets! We've run into a war!"

"We didn't know they were making movies in here," said Ricky.

Before the actor could reply, another man, dressed in shorts, a sport shirt, cap, and dark glasses stepped onto the trail.

"Don't be too hard on those kids," he said and then introduced himself as Victor Grattan. "I'm the director of this movie," he said. "How would you fellows like to look around?"

"But—" Regente spluttered.

"Don't be such a prima donna, Alexis," the director said. "Besides, we're taking a break for an hour."

"Thank you," Teddy said. "We didn't mean to do any harm."

"Oh, I know that," the director replied. Then he led them into a vast clearing. In the middle stood a temple pyramid, a crumbling ruin, half-covered by jungle growth.

Men in ancient Mayan garb walked about, and two cameras, mounted on high platforms, were aimed down at the scene.

"Alexis is temperamental," Grattan said, still apologizing for his leading man. He told the boys that the company was from Hollywood and that they were making location shots for a movie called *The Mystery of the Mayas.*

"In the script," the man went on, "we discover an ancient temple filled with gems and valuable relics."

85

"Why, that's just like the place we—" Ricky silenced himself under the disapproving eyes of Pete and Teddy.

"What's that you were saying?" the director asked.

"Nothing," Ricky mumbled.

Pete noticed that people in regular clothes were going out of a small doorway at the foot of the pyramid. Some carried baskets on their backs, others lugged small burlap sacks.

"They're setting up props for another scene," the director explained, and led the boys over to where a small crane was placed over a hole in the ground.

"It's an old storage well," Grattan said. "We're exploring it. Would you like to go down and have a look?" He winked at Pete.

"Is it possible?"

"Of course," the director replied. He motioned to a man sitting in the crane, and a cable with a belt attached to the end swung down to where the boys were standing.

Before Pete could say yes, no, or maybe, the director attached the belt around his waist, and motioned again to the operator.

The motor chugged and Pete suddenly felt himself lifted off the ground. Then the crane operator lowered the boy through the hole. Down, down he went, into the blackness.

"I should have taken a flashlight," Pete said to himself. "I can't see anything."

Finally his feet rested on something mucky and slimy.

"I'm at the bottom!" he called up to the tiny hole of light far above his head.

He tried to take a step, but slipped and nearly fell in the ooze. "I hope they pull me up soon," he thought.

But nothing happened. After a few minutes, a voice called down, "Sorry! The pulley broke. We can't get you out!"

CHAPTER 10

PINK TOENAILS

A SHIVER went through Pete. Was he to be a prisoner in the old well?

"It may take a day to fix this," the voice came again.

Pete stepped to one side to get a better look up to the opening and felt something slither against his right foot.

"Help! Help!" Pete cried out in alarm. "Get me out of here!" Just then he felt pressure on his belt. He was lifted off the floor of the old cistern and began a slow ascent up the black hole. When he got to the top, he squinted his eyes against the bright sun. Much to his surprise he heard the director laughing.

"That gave you a scare, didn't it?" the man asked. "I was just joking."

"It wasn't funny," said Pete.

"No, it wasn't," Teddy chimed in. "You should not have done that."

Now Alexis Regente, minus his plumed headgear, walked over, grinning. "We always play practical jokes. You'll get used to that if you stay around here long enough," he said.

"But I'm afraid the boys can't stay very long today," the director put in. "As a matter of fact we usually don't allow guests on location."

"Then, you mean, we can't come back again?" asked Ricky, taken by the colorful costumes of the actors.

"Well, seeing that you're Americans, I guess you can," the director said, smiling. "Make it day after tomorrow."

The cousins retraced their steps into the woods, followed the railroad tracks, and then turned off toward the hacienda. Going up the drive they saw their mothers beside the pool in swimsuits and the girls splashing in the water.

Ricky raced ahead. "Wait'll you hear what happened to us!" he shouted. "Was it great!"

"What?" said Holly, climbing out the pool. The other girls hastened after her.

"You look excited," said Pam. "Hurry up and tell us."

Ricky's eyes flashed with mischief. "Just be patient, ladies," he said very slowly.

Holly put her hands on her hips. "You tell us right this minute, Ricky Hollister, or I'll drip on you."

"Okay, okay," he said, backing up, as Pete and Teddy arrived. "Just listen."

The three boys told their adventure and the rest of the family was amazed.

"But it's a funny thing," Pete said. "There weren't any girls in the cast."

Pam recalled reading about ritual dances, which were done entirely by the Mayan men. "Maybe that's the reason you didn't see any girls," she said.

The swimmers left to dress for supper. The four girls shared a large bedroom at the end of the portico, next to the boys' room, which was beside their mothers'.

Jean was ready first and stood at the window looking down the drive. "Maybe Daddy will come tonight," she said to the others. "Let's watch for him."

In their crisp, fresh cottons the cousins strolled to the gateway and waited hopefully, but Uncle Russ did not come.

After supper they met Balám in the lobby. He too was impatient to start searching for the Temple of the Laughing Idol. Yes, he said he had heard about the movie company, but the natives did not like the actors. "They order everybody around," Balám complained, "as if they owned Yucatán."

A little later, Pam and Jean slipped off to Yotam's house. Tomás was not there, and the little girl was playing with a neighbor child, who ran off when he saw the visitors.

"Where's Tomás?" asked Pam.

The girl looked up with soulful eyes and pointed into the jungle.

"Let's follow where he went," said Jean.

"*Yo tam hai*," said Yotam, and the cousins laughed. The Mayan child took Pam's hand and led her to a little path which went into the forest. Tall trees nearly blacked out the sunshine as they pressed deeper through the brush.

Suddenly somebody jumped up from behind a tree, making Jean cry out in fright.

It was Tomás. He seemed angry. "Why are you following me?" he asked. "Go back!"

"We're taking a walk," Pam spoke up.

"It's dangerous here," Tomás said. "There's a witch nearby."

Jean waved her hand at him and replied, "Oh, pooh! There aren't any witches!"

The boy did not answer, but wheeled about and disappeared again.

"It's getting too dark to follow him now," Pam said and suggested that they go back. They had taken only a few steps, when they heard a tap-tap-tap sound coming from the forest.

Yotam grasped Pam's hand tightly and raced along the trail until she came to her house. The cousins said good-by there and returned to the hacienda.

"That Tomás is up to something," said Pam, as they prepared for bed that evening.

"What do you mean?" asked Holly and the two older girls told about the forest trip.

"If it's a mystery, Pam'll solve it, I know," said Jean.

Next morning, after the Hollisters had finished breakfast, little Yotam met Pam at the dining room door. "Here, I have a *presente* for you," she said.

She raised her hand and offered the gift. It looked like a small wooden beetle attached to a thread, with a pin at the end of it.

Yotam fixed the pin to Pam's blouse.

Sue skipped over to watch what was going on, as Pam said to Yotam, "Did you make that yourself?"

All at once Sue let out a scream. "The beetle's alive!"

Pam glanced down and saw the creature moving over her blouse. "Ugh!" she cried. "Get it off me!"

Yotam looked at her, very surprised. "The beetle will not hurt you," she said.

"Won't it bite?" Pam asked, making a face as she kept her eyes on the little black bug.

Just then the waitress poked her head out of the door and, with an amused look, said, "The bug is harmless. It is a custom with our children to have live beetle pins."

Hearing this, Pam thanked Yotam for the gift, and walked around showing everybody her new pin.

"Let me wear it for a while," little Sue begged.

Pam gave her sister the pin, and Sue scooted away to the place where Holly had put Tan-Tan's cage under a low green bush. She bent down, opened the top of the cage, and took the chicken in her arms.

"Look what I have, Tan-Tan," she said.

Tan-Tan looked at the little bug. Like lightning, her neck darted forward.

The chicken's neck darted forward.

Peck! Peck! And the bug was gone!

Sue burst into tears. She ran back to her sister, still holding the chicken in her arms. "Ow, ow," she cried. "Pam, your bug pin is ruined!"

When Pam told Yotam what had happened, the little girl said, "I'll make you another," and hurried off.

Hearing about the sad end of the decorative bug, Mrs. Hollister said, "Susie, what would you like to do, go swimming with us, or play with Tan-Tan?"

Although the youngster was provoked by Tan-Tan's eating habits, she decided to play with her chicken. While the others donned their swimsuits and frolicked in the pool, Sue took her pet into her mother's bedroom. On the dresser she saw a bottle of nail polish marked Peachy Pink.

"I know what I'll do," the little girl thought, glancing at Tan-Tan's little yellow feet. "I'll paint her toenails." She had trouble opening the bottle but finally the cap came loose. Then, sitting on the side of her mother's bed, holding the chicken in her left arm, Sue painted the long toenails. The chicken squirmed and fussed, but Sue held her tightly.

"How pretty," the girl murmured. "Pink and yellow look so nice together."

Then she hastened to the pool's edge, showing everyone who would look the beautiful pink toenails on Tan-Tan.

"Oh, Susie," Mrs. Hollister said, pulling herself up, dripping wet, to the side of the pool. "What have you done!"

Pam popped her head out of the water, flung her hair back, and laughed.

"Why didn't you paint her yellow beak, too?"

"Oh, I'll do that right now!" Sue said.

"No!" cried her mother. "Sue, come back here this minute! You will not paint any more of that poor bird!"

Sue put Tan-Tan on the ground and the chicken picked among the blades of grass looking for more insects to eat.

After lunch Sue continued to play with Tan-Tan. She and Holly were sitting on the side patio next to the road, trying to make the chicken hop over their hands, when they heard the noise of a truck around a bend in the road.

Tucking Tan-Tan under her arm, Holly got up to look. She exclaimed: "That's the same truck that hit us, Sue!" Indeed, it was the same, dusty, green truck, again loaded high with crates. The driver, too, looked familiar.

"Let's give him back the chicken," said Sue, who was really growing a little tired of Tan-Tan. She ran into the middle of the street and flung up her hands for the truck to stop. The driver shouted as the brakes screeched!

CHAPTER 11

BREAD ON THE HEAD

THE TRUCK jerked to a stop barely three feet in front of Sue.

Holly grabbed her frightened sister by the hand and pulled her out of the road.

"Sue," she said, "never, NEVER do that again."

The child's chin quivered. "I'm sorry."

"Mommy's told you a thousand times," said Holly sternly.

"I forgot," Sue murmured.

"Well, you *can't* forget," scolded Holly. As she spoke, she became aware of a loud squawking. In her fright she had forgotten that she was still clutching the chicken under one arm.

"You're hurting her," said Sue, sniffling.

"I'm sorry. I was squeezing her awful tight, 'cause I was so scared." She noticed then that the truck was driving away.

"Wait!" Holly shouted. "Take your chicken!"

Grabbing Sue's hand, she started to run after the pickup, but it did not stop.

"Was that Señor Punto driving?" asked Holly breathlessly.

"It looked like him," said Sue.

The sisters trotted along the road, hoping that the driver would stop and claim the chicken.

"Mother would want us to give it back," said Holly, "'cause that's the right thing to do."

But the truck kept going, and soon it turned off to the right.

Holly slowed down. "He's not going to stop," she said, disgusted. "I think that's mean. Even if he didn't hear me call, he must have seen us in his rear-view mirror."

"Pam says Señor Punto might be a bad man," Sue declared.

Holly's eyes narrowed. "I'll tell you what! Let's see if we can find out where he went."

She hefted the chicken into a firmer position and they hiked up the road until they came to the spot where the truck disappeared. A narrow trail, only a car's width, led them through a deep tangle of jungle, heavily laced with vines and branches. The girls stopped and looked about.

"I wonder where this leads to," Holly said, twirling one of her pigtails. The girls walked along, cautiously glancing left and right. Fifty feet from the main road, the trail forked. The left branch was narrower, so the sisters selected the right-hand one, thinking that the truck might have gone down there. Deeper and deeper into the forest they pressed.

"Here, you take Tan-Tan for a while," said Holly. She handed the hen to her sister, but as she did, the little girl tripped on a vine and fell face down.

97

Tan-Tan squawked, flapped her wings, and flew off into the jungle.

Sue lay on the ground and did not rise.

"What's the matter, are you hurt?" asked Holly, bending down. The smaller girl did not reply, but kept her face close to a sandy spot in the tall grass.

"Look what I see!" Sue whispered.

Holly dropped on hands and knees to observe a small cone-shaped hole in the sand. A tiny bug was digging down in the bottom of it. Then it disappeared.

"I wonder where he went," said Sue. As she spoke, an unwary ant slipped down one side of the hole and when it reached the bottom, *chump chump!* the hidden bug popped up and ate it.

The girls watched silently for several minutes, as two more ants entered the trap and were promptly devoured by the bug.

Sue frowned. "I think it's terrible," she declared. "Tan-Tan ate Pam's little bug and now this bug is eating littler bugs."

Holly shrugged. "Everything's got to eat."

Fascinated, the girls watched a while longer. They were about to rise when they heard men's voices. Holly gestured Sue to be quiet.

"It might be Señor Punto," the pigtailed girl whispered. The sisters crept into higher grass and lay still.

"But I can't see anything," Sue protested.

"Shh—listen to what they're saying."

The words that reached their ears were spoken in good English, and apparently came from two men. One of them said, "We've searched everywhere and can't find it."

"I know," said his companion, "and if one of those kids gets wind of this, the game is up."

There was silence for a few moments, then the first fellow said, "Then I say, get Hollister and his map! We've got to find the Laughing Idol before he does!"

The men's voices became indistinct. Quickly the girls lifted their heads in order to see who the men were, but only glimpsed their backs as they disappeared deeper into the jungle.

"Oh dear," Holly said. "They were talking about Uncle Russ. Those men know all about the Laughing Idol!"

"What do we do?" Sue asked.

"Get home as fast as we can, that's what," Holly said. She reached for her sister's hand and they made their way back along the trail.

"We ought to be to the road by now," declared Sue, glancing up at treetops, which spread like a gloomy canopy over their heads.

They walked on for another ten minutes, with the idea gradually dawning upon them that they were lost!

"What'll we do?" asked Sue in a quavering voice.

Holly bit her lip and did not answer. They might have to spend all night in the dark jungle!

Suddenly they heard a noise in the thicket and glanced about to see a native girl, about eight years old. She wore a *huipil* and carried a chicken in her arms.

"That's Tan-Tan," said Holly, noticing the pink toenails.

The girl disappeared like a shadow, and Sue began to cry. Then the little native reappeared and beckoned.

"We're lost," said Holly. "Will you please show us the way back to the hacienda?"

The native girl shook her head, indicating that she did not speak English, but again beckoned for the two to follow her.

They tramped through the woods about a quarter of a mile until they came to an Indian village in a clearing. The small brown huts looked like big chocolate bonbons.

The girl went into one of the larger huts, about which nine young children were playing. She came out with a stout smiling native woman. Her hair was pulled back in a tight bun and she too wore a *huipil*. Beside her walked a small thin man.

The native girl indicated that the couple were her mother and father and the children her sisters and brothers.

Eagerly she showed them the chicken with the pink toenails, and the children crowded about curiously, babbling and touching the painted feet.

"Maybe they never saw nail polish before," Holly whispered to her sister.

"Will you help us reach home?" she asked the Mayan woman. She did not understand.

Again and again the children tried to find out from the native couple how to reach Hacienda Copal, but they only shrugged and smiled. Then the woman kindly gestured that the Hollisters could sleep with them overnight.

"Oh, no, we can't do that," said Holly. "Mother will worry about us too much."

Just then some of the children ran shouting toward a man who was walking into the village. He wore sandals, baggy blue trousers, a white sport shirt, and a straw hat. On his head he carried the funniest thing!

It was a huge, white tin container, about two feet in diameter, and had a top shaped like a cone.

He walked very straight, balancing the can as if it were no trouble at all.

Holly and Sue ran over to him, crying out, "Please, do you speak English?"

"*Sí, un poco*," the man said. He smiled at them with gleaming white teeth and added, "Manuel speak a lee-tle English."

"What is that thing on your head?" asked Sue.

The man removed the container and set it on the ground. Then he opened the top, and the children saw that it was full of small loaves of bread.

"Please, do you speak English?"

"I am bread man," Manuel said. "I bake and sell to villagers."

"Then you know where Hacienda Copal is?" Holly asked. "That's where we're staying."

As the natives reached down for the bread they would purchase, the baker cocked his head and looked at the Hollisters. "You are long way from home, but I will take you back."

"Oh, goody!" said Sue, dancing up and down and clapping her hands.

"Would you like to eat some of my bread?" the baker offered.

The girls eyed the crusty loaves hungrily. The man smiled. "Go ahead—it is a *presente.*"

"Thank you," said Holly and Sue together. After eating a loaf, Holly said, "It was yummy." Then she added, "Would you do me a favor?"

"*Sí, sí.*"

"I'd like to balance that thingamajig on my head. Is it hard to do?"

"No," came the reply, and the smiling baker reached down, picked up the bread container and placed it on the girl's head.

Holly rolled her eyes, and tried to hold her head still as she began to walk.

"Ha, you've got a flat head!" said Sue.

Holly giggled. "Don't make me laugh!"

Just then the huge tin tilted to one side and slid off Holly's head!

CHAPTER 12

SUSPICIOUS POTATOES

BEFORE Holly had time to move, an Indian boy leaped to her side and caught the falling bread tin. He grinned, showing white teeth, then put the container on top of his own head and strode around in circles, flapping his arms like a bird.

Everybody laughed. "That's great," said Holly and turned to the baker. "Tell him he's good."

With Manuel as translator, Holly and Sue were soon carrying on a lively conversation with the village children.

Holly told the little girl that she could keep the chicken. The Mayans looked pleased. Then Holly suddenly remembered why she and Sue had become lost, and inquired whether the natives had seen a man who looked like Señor Punto.

The girl's father looked fearfully at his wife, who briefly answered. Manuel said, "She does not like to talk about it. There has been a bad luck sign."

When the girls seemed confused, he told them a strange story. One of the Mayan children had seen a green vine snake in the morning. It was very long and thin as a pencil. "But it wouldn't bite anybody," Manuel said.

"Then why is it unlucky?" asked Holly.

The breadman explained: "If someone sees a green vine snake on Tuesday, he must follow the snake, catch it, and cut it into nine pieces!"

"Ugh!" declared Sue, putting both hands in front of her eyes.

"Nine is a magic number to us," Manuel continued. "If the snake is not killed and cut in nine pieces, the one who sees it will die in two years."

"I don't believe it," Holly declared. "But what's that got to do with the men in the woods?"

Manuel said that the snake had disappeared near where two strangers had been seen. "That means those men would bring bad luck," he went on.

Holly looked around at the silent Indians. "But —" she said.

"No use," the baker put in quickly. "They won't talk."

Then he glanced up at the sky and said, "Come, it's getting late. I will take you to Hacienda Copal." The girls and he said good-by to the Mayan Indians and set off briskly through the jungle over a narrow trail which he knew well.

The sisters were full of questions, and when Sue asked about the strange little bug which ate the ants, Manuel laughed. "That was a doodlebug," he said, then asked, "Have you ever heard of the army ants?"

"Army ants?" asked Holly, being careful not to

trip on the roots along the darkening path. "I thought only men went in the army."

Manuel told them that just before the rainy season starts, a whole army of ants roams through the jungle. There were millions of them, devouring other insects, mice, lizards, anything in their way.

"And what about the villages?" asked Sue. "Do they eat up all the children, too?"

"The villagers get out of the way," said Manuel, "and let the ants right through their huts. They eat garbage, bugs, everything, and when they leave, the villages are clean!"

"Just like spring housecleaning," said Holly. Then she stopped suddenly.

"Listen!" She had heard a rustling in the bushes beside the trail.

The three stood still for a moment in the gloomy forest. Once again the noise came and a bush stirred.

Holly took a deep breath and parted the leaves. Two frightened brown faces looked out at her.

"It's boys!" exclaimed Sue. Each carried a sack on his back supported by a strap which went around his forehead.

Like startled rabbits the two scrambled free and began to push into the brush!

"Wait!" cried Holly. "Oh, Manuel, quick, make them stop. Say you'll give 'em some bread!"

The man called and the boys stopped. After a moment they returned shyly. Holly, who had a ten-

Two frightened brown faces looked out.

cent piece in her pocket, gave it to the baker and he handed each boy a small loaf.

"Ask them why they were hiding," said Holly. But the boys would not answer the question.

"What are they carrying in their sacks?" asked Sue.

"*Papa*," one of the boys replied.

"They look like potatoes," was Holly's comment.

"*Sí, papa*, potatoes, the same thing," Manuel explained.

As the boys munched the bread, Holly kept wondering why they had hidden and tried to run off. "Maybe they are carrying something else in their sacks," she thought, and tried to peek into the burlap bags.

The boys backed away. "*Papa*," they said. "*Papa*." With that they disappeared into the jungle.

The two girls and their guide pressed on and soon reached a road not far from Hacienda Copal. Pete was the first to see them. He shouted the news of their return and word spread quickly throughout the hacienda. Everyone hastened out to greet the two lost girls, who quickly told the story of their rescue by Manuel.

"You must take a reward," Mrs. Hollister told the bread man.

But he held up his hand and turned his head. "No. I only did it to help."

When he was gone and the other onlookers had left, Mrs. Hollister took the two girls into her room, seated herself on the bed and looked at them sternly.

"Everyone has been very worried about you."

Sue hung her head.

"Please, Mother," said Holly bravely, "don't blame Sue. It was all my idea."

"Both of you should know better than to go off like that without permission—especially you, Holly, because you're older and I've told you a thousand times."

Sue sneaked a look at her sister whose face went beet red. "We won't do it again," said Holly.

"All right," said Mrs. Hollister. She drew them close and gave each one a kiss. "Now we'll go to the dining room. Dinner is over, but the cook has saved a nice meal for you."

While the girls ate hungrily, the rest of the family sat around questioning them about their adventure.

When Aunt Marge heard what the two men had said, she became excited. "Goodness! They're after Russ! Oh, I hope he gets here soon."

Shortly after they had eaten, Holly and Sue went drowsily to their bedroom and fell fast asleep.

Pete, Pam, Ricky, and their cousins, however, sat in the moonlit patio talking about their mystery. Balám had returned to Chichén Itzá for the day. Would he and Uncle Russ believe it was too dangerous now to pursue the quest of the Laughing Idol?

"I don't think so," said Pam. "They're brave men."

Seeing the moonlight reflected in the rippling water of the pool, Pete snapped his fingers. "Let's have a moonlight swim!" he said.

"Will it be all right?" asked Pam.

"Sure, if we don't make any noise," said Teddy.

The children went quietly to their rooms. Pete dropped his dungarees onto the floor and pulled on his swim trunks. Then he returned to the pool, where the others waited for him. One by one they slid into the pool and swam quietly about.

"Crickets, this is great," said Pete.

Ricky floated on his back, spouting water between his teeth like a whale.

After the children had swum for a while, Pam suddenly said, "Look, who's that walking past our room?"

The others glanced up to see a white figure disappearing at the far end of the portico.

"I don't know," replied Jean.

"Whoever it was," Pam said, "came out of your room, Pete."

Suddenly a chill snaked along Pete's spine! He had left his dungarees and the belt with the secret compartment unguarded!

He pulled himself out of the pool and raced toward the portico. The others followed, toweling briskly.

Pete dashed into his moonlit room and glanced on the floor where he had left his dungarees.

They had vanished!

"The map! It's been stolen!" Pete gasped.

CHAPTER 13

A SCORPION SCARE

PETE's cry of alarm brought the other swimmers running into his bedroom. Mrs. Hollister and his aunt followed from their room next door. With his swimming trunks still dripping, Pete hastily told of the disappearance of his dungarees and the belt holding the secret map.

His mother and Aunt Marge were shocked to hear it.

"It's terrible!" his aunt said. "This mystery is getting more puzzling all the time!"

"We'll take care of you, Mother," Teddy said bravely.

"Are you sure the dungarees weren't kicked under the bed?" asked Jean.

"Come on, let's look!" said Pam. She got down on hands and knees to peer under the bed. "There, I see something."

"The dungarees?" Ricky asked excitedly.

"No," Pam said. She bent her head beneath the bed and stretched her right hand toward a black object. "It looks like a bug!" the girl said, wriggling closer.

Suddenly a woman's voice cried out, "Don't touch it!"

Pam shrank back, crawled out from under the bed to face the hacienda housekeeper. She was a stout Mayan lady, who spoke Spanish and English as well as her own tongue.

"Boys," she said with a nod to Pete and Teddy, "help me move the bed."

It was pushed from the wall, and there lay a creature which looked to the children like a crayfish.

"That's a scorpion," the housekeeper said. "I'm awful sorry that it got into your bedroom."

"Will it bite?" asked Holly.

"Yes," came the reply. "Scorpions are very dangerous." The woman hastened out and shortly returned with a brown paper bag and a dust brush. Soon the dangerous insect was captured.

Now it occurred to Pete that they still had to search for the missing dungarees. When he told the story to the housekeeper, she said, "That white figure you saw must have been the maid. She was taking things to the laundry. We run our own here at night, you know."

"We'll look there right away," said Pete.

"I'll go with you," offered Teddy.

"All right," said Mrs. Hollister, "but the rest of you had better hop into your pajamas and call it a night."

The housekeeper directed the boys to a small building behind the hacienda. In the distance they could hear the faint churn of the washing machines, and see a plume of steam coming from a pipe in the roof.

As the cousins hastened along a concrete walk toward the laundry, Teddy glanced toward the crafts shop and seized Pete by the arm, whirling him around.

A thin man, a hat pulled low over his eyes, was slipping out of the front door, with a box in his hand.

Without a moment's hesitation the boys raced toward him. The fellow ducked among the palm trees and thick tropical shrubs and was gone.

"He must have headed toward the road," Teddy said, and the two boys raced in that direction. But there was no man to be seen, nor even a car in which he might have escaped.

"We'd better tell Mr. and Mrs. Rico about this right away," said Pete, retracing his steps past the swimming pool and down the stairs to the Indian settlement. Approaching the Ricos' hut, Pete called out to them, and soon the crafts shop owner and his wife came out of the open doorway.

After hearing the boys' report, they ran toward their shop.

There they found that the small lock, which secured the flimsy door, had been broken. The couple hastened inside and turned on a light. Mrs. Rico gasped.

"The Wise Men!" she said. "A whole box of Wise Men has been stolen!"

"They're very valuable," Mr. Rico said, and shook his head sadly.

He told Pete and Teddy that the little statuettes of Gaspar, Melchor, and Baltasar were beautifully hand-painted and much in demand by tourists.

Then Pete told about his missing dungarees, and the Ricos offered to help search the laundry with the cousins.

As they entered the building, the boys smelled the aroma of soap and steam. A maid in a white uniform was bending over a huge pile of clothes next to the door, sorting them before their trip to the washing machine.

On the opposite side, toward the rear of the building, three other women were busy ironing. The maid stood up and gave the two boys a surprised look.

"Did you take a pair of dungarees from my room—number six?" Pete asked.

The woman smiled, and replied, "Sí, sí," pointing to the large washing machine.

"They're being washed now," Teddy said.

"But what about the belt?" Pete said. "Did you see it?"

The maid nodded and beckoned to the boys, leading them to a small closet. She opened the door. There on a hook was the belt.

"Thanks a lot," said Pete. He took it down, stepped aside and felt for the map. All safe!

"Phew!" He gave a sigh of relief and grinned at his cousin.

Meanwhile Teddy had kept the maid's attention. "Thank you again," he said. "That's a very valuable belt."

The Ricos too were happy that it had not been lost.

As the four turned to leave, Pete accidentally stepped on the pile of laundry. His foot hit a hard object, and a muffled grunt followed. Then something moved at the bottom of the pile!

Startled, Pete jumped aside.

"Who—who's there?" the boy called out, and the others turned around to see what was happening.

Suddenly, out of the shirts, shorts, handkerchiefs and *huipils* came a brown hand! Then a thin man sprang up. In his other hand he held the box of stolen statuettes.

"Punto's friend!" Pete thought. "Vargas!"

For an instant everyone froze in surprise. Then the thief dropped the box on the pile of soft clothing and dashed for the door. But an *huipil* had caught on his feet and he stumbled and fell flat.

Pete and Teddy made a dive for him, but he slithered out of the way. Freeing himself from the dress, he jumped up and hurled it at the boys' heads.

For a moment they were blinded by the big garment. Then they tore it off and raced after the fugitive.

Everyone froze in surprise.

Through the hacienda grounds they zigzagged, hot on his heels. Behind them they could hear the shouts of the Ricos and the maids screaming.

Suddenly as they rounded the swimming pool, Teddy slipped on a wet spot. SPLASH! He skidded headlong into the water.

But Pete kept running, gaining on the man as they reached the road. A car was coming! The fugitive ran toward it, waving his arms wildly.

Half blinded by the headlights, Pete pounded after the man. "He's crazy!" the boy thought. "If he stops this car, he'll get caught!"

As he ran, Pete heard a clamor over his shoulder and looked back to see Teddy, dripping wet, with the hotel manager, two maids, and another male guest.

There was a screech of brakes as the oncoming vehicle careened to a stop.

It was the chicken truck!

The man at the wheel yelled something in Spanish and the fugitive tried to climb aboard.

"No you don't!" gasped Pete. He made a flying tackle and yanked the fellow off the truck. The two fell to the road, rolling over and over into a ditch.

The pickup roared off and was nearly out of sight when Teddy and the others reached Pete and his struggling captive. Mr. Cortez pulled the man roughly to his feet and demanded his name.

"It's Vargas," said Teddy, and told what little

they knew of the man. The culprit glowered but would not talk.

"We'll lock you in one of our rooms, until the police can come for you tomorrow morning!" the manager said. "No need to bother them this late."

Everyone in the hacienda was awake and talking excitedly as the prisoner was tied hand and foot and put into a storage room on the first floor. There was only one high window and the door was locked.

Then the boys took the family aside and quietly reported finding the map.

"Oh," Mrs. Hollister sighed, "I hope this means our troubles are over."

As the Hollisters returned to bed, they heard the guests praising the two boys for their part in the capture of the thief.

"Yikes," said Ricky, "why didn't they call me? I could have helped 'em catch that fellow."

"The trouble isn't over yet," said Teddy as he and Pete followed the others along the portico. "Vargas is more than a sneak thief. I'll bet he and Punto are after the Laughing Idol temple."

Pete agreed. "And don't forget the two English-speaking fellows Holly overheard. They might all be part of the same gang."

Teddy nodded. "Maybe the police will be able to get something out of Vargas in the morning."

As they reached their room, Teddy stopped short, his hand on the doorknob. "Oh no!" he exclaimed softly. "Pete, I've made a terrible boo-boo."

"What do you mean?"

"In the laundry. When I said your belt was so valuable—Vargas may have heard me. He might guess the map is in it. Or just be interested in stealing the belt for its own sake."

"Why worry," said Pete. "He's out of circulation now."

"But he might find a way to pass the word on to his pals."

"I'll be extra careful," said Pete with a chuckle. "I'll wear it in bed."

The next morning Pete was shaken awake by Ricky. He swung his feet over the side of the bed and blinked at Teddy, who also had been awakened by the redhead.

Teddy yawned and stretched. "Why'd you wake us up so early, Ricky?"

"To show you my muscle."

"What?" said Pete. "You woke us up for that?"

Ricky said he had done a few push-ups the evening before, and was sure that his muscles had developed greatly. He skinned off his pajama tops, flexed his right arm and looked at his biceps. The muscle rose ever so slightly.

"Come on, get up there!" Ricky said, urging his muscles. Then he turned his head and looked at his left arm. "I guess maybe it was this one."

Teddy and Pete could not help bursting out laughing, but Ricky's embarrassment was short-lived.

For several doors away, the boys heard Sue's shrill voice:

"Mommy! Come here quick! Aunt Marge, hurry!"

CHAPTER 14

A SHARP ARROW

HEADS popped out of doors to see whether the little girl was in some kind of trouble. But Sue was all smiles. The early morning sun glistened off her shiny black hair and she gestured wildly.

"Uncle Russ! He's here!" She dashed toward the place where cars were parked. The boys quickly dressed and followed. Then the women and the girl cousins arrived to see Uncle Russ taking his luggage out of a shiny red sports car.

Balám was with him. The Mayan guide walked around the automobile, admiring it.

After Jean and Teddy had been hugged by their father, Aunt Marge threw her arms around him. "We thought you'd never get here," she said joyfully.

"I was delayed on some business," Uncle Russ said. "When I arrived in Mérida, I ran into Balám, and we rented this car."

"Uncle Russ! Uncle Russ!" Holly broke in. "We've caught a bad man!"

"What? Really?"

The excited children poured out the story. "His name is Vargas," said Pam. "He's a tall thin man and . . ." Suddenly she stopped as an idea hit her.

"Thin man!" she repeated. "Uncle Russ! Maybe he's Aguila!"

"I can soon tell you," said her uncle. "Where is he?"

The cartoonist was quickly taken to the room which had served for a jail overnight and Mr. Cortez was called. The manager turned the key in the lock.

"Take a look at him," he said to Uncle Russ as he opened the door. "Maybe you can recognize the fellow!"

Suddenly everyone gasped. The room was empty! The two pieces of rope lay on the floor, and there were toe marks against the wall, showing that the thief had escaped through the window.

"Come on!" said Pam. "Maybe he just got away and is in the back now!"

The children raced around the hacienda. Beneath the window they found the shrubbery broken by the fugitive's leap. But he was nowhere to be seen.

His trail, however, led to the road and Pam said, "Maybe that truck hid nearby and waited for him to escape."

"More likely the driver came back," Pete said, "climbed in the window, and helped Vargas get out."

"I'll bet that driver was Señor Punto!" declared Jean.

"You know him, Uncle Russ?" asked Pam eagerly.

"Never heard of him," said the cartoonist. "Balám told me about him and his pal."

"You're sure Skeets Packer never mentioned Punto?" said Pete.

His uncle thought for a moment. "I'm sure he didn't."

A babble of excited voices broke out. "Easy now! Easy!" said Russ Hollister. "Suppose we sit down somewhere, and you start this story from the beginning."

When the cartoonist's baggage had been taken in, he sat down on a chair in the patio and the family surrounded him, telling all about what had happened since they had arrived in Yucatán.

"This really is something," Uncle Russ said, and his eyes twinkled. "What a great subject for my comic strip!"

"Will we be in it too?" asked Holly.

"Of course," Uncle Russ replied. "All of you, but I'll have to use different names."

Just then Balám beckoned to Uncle Russ, who excused himself, saying they would discuss their plans at lunch. Then he went off with the Mayan guide to make preparations for the trip into the jungle.

The children went to watch the Ricos painting figurines in the crafts shop. The man told them that they had recovered the box of Wise Men safely from the laundry pile. He and his wife thanked Pete and Teddy warmly. Mrs. Rico insisted on giving each child a little figure of a Mayan Indian.

Embarrassed, they thanked the couple, then left to put on swimsuits and slip into the pool.

When lunchtime came, Aunt Marge and Mrs. Hollister reserved a large table in one corner of the dining room. Uncle Russ sat at the head of the table, and soon conversation turned to the Yucatán mystery. Uncle Russ said that he had contacted the police, and that Señor Punto was as much of a puzzle to them as he was to him.

"He's up to no good, I'm sure of that," the cartoonist said. The police, he added, were constantly on the alert for ancient objects which were being stolen from the temples of Yucatán.

"Señor Punto wants you to lead him to the Temple of the Laughing Idol," said Pam. "Then he can rob it!"

"And if he could get the secret map," said Pete, "he might go there directly himself."

"Those two would steal anything that wasn't nailed down, I bet," said Ricky. "It wouldn't surprise me if one of them stole the ring from me. Punto knew I had it."

While they were speaking, two men entered the dining room and took seats within earshot of the Hollisters. Immediately Pete lowered his voice.

"You can't be too careful," Teddy remarked softly. "Those fellows might be trying to eavesdrop on us."

"Oh, no," Pam said sympathetically. "Look, they're speaking the sign language."

The Hollisters had once met a deaf boy in Shoreham, and he had helped them solve a mystery. Ever since then, the children had felt a special sympathy for people who could not hear.

Certain that the diners were not able to listen to the conversation, Uncle Russ talked about their trip into the jungle.

"That map is all important," he said. "Pete, I think we'd better make a duplicate of it. I'll carry the original in my wallet, and you can keep the copy in the secret compartment of your belt."

After lunch was over, Pete and Teddy got some tracing paper from the hacienda office and in a short time had made a copy of the map. Then they gave the original to Uncle Russ, who tucked it into the billfold compartment of his wallet.

Pam and Jean, meanwhile, had their heads together in the shade of a palm tree where both were seated at a small table. Before them was a tablet of paper with letters and numbers on it.

"What are you doing there?" asked Pete, putting the duplicate map into his belt.

Jean beckoned the boys over and said in a low voice, "We're making a secret code!"

"What do we need that for?" asked Teddy and bent over the sheet of paper.

Pam explained that since their journey into the jungle would be dangerous, they might possibly need to send a secret message. "We want one that no-body will understand," she said.

"That's a good idea," Pete agreed. The Shore-ham youngsters had made a secret code before, and it often came in handy on detective cases.

On the table lay a book on Yucatán, opened at a page which gave the names of the months and the days.

"Here's what we worked out," said Pam. She took the eighteen months and ran the letters to-gether in four lines of eighteen characters.

POPUOZIPZOTZTZECXU

LYAXKINMOLCHENYAXZ

ACCEHMACKANKINMUAN

PAXKAYABCUMHUUAYEB

"Where do you get a code out of that?" asked Teddy.

"It's simple," his sister replied. "Take the name Pam. P is in the first line. It is also the first letter. So it's represented by one over one.

"And A," said Jean, "comes in the second line and is the third letter. That would be two over three. The M occurs in the second line, and the eighth letter, that's two over eight."

"Oh, I see," said Pete. "It looks like arithmetic, but it really isn't."

Pam was quick to add that some letters were not included in the code. "So that'll make it even harder for someone to guess," she said.

Pam and Jean made four copies and each of the cousins took a code. They planned to tell Ricky and Holly about it later.

"Everybody take a pencil, too," said Jean, pushing several toward them. "Mr. Cortez said we could have these."

After they had returned the book and tablet to the manager, they went to the patio. There Mrs. Hollister walked over to them. "Aren't you forgetting something today?" she asked.

"No, what?" said Pete.

"I thought you were going to watch the movies being made."

"Crickets!" he exclaimed. "So much has been going on here, I clean forgot about that!"

"Maybe all the shooting has been done for the day," Teddy said.

"Come on, we'd better hurry if we want to see anything!" Ricky said.

Mrs. Hollister and Aunt Marge decided to stay behind and Sue needed her afternoon nap.

"But I'd feel much better if Uncle Russ went with you," Mrs. Hollister said.

The youngsters found the cartoonist in his room with Balám, sharpening two long knives.

"These are machetes," the cartoonist said. "We'll have to hack our way into the thick jungle with them."

"Please come with us to see the movies now," begged Holly.

Uncle Russ said he would be glad to go. Balám, though, would stay behind to gather supplies for their jungle trip. In a few minutes the sightseers set out to find the little railroad line that would lead them to the movie makers.

When they reached the area, Pete was surprised to hear the strange bird again.

"That must be one that lives in the deep woods," he remarked. "I never heard it around the hacienda."

Soon an actor, adjusting his warrior's uniform, appeared out of the woods.

"We've been waiting for you," he said. "Just about to do some interesting shooting."

The visitors were guided to the large area before the ancient temple. The cameras were working as "slaves" laden with brown sacks filed out of the pyramid ruins.

Holly tugged at her older brother. "Look at those sacks. That's the same kind the boys were carrying potatoes in," she said.

Before Pete could reply, Victor Grattan approached them. "You came just in time to see a marvelous scene," he said. "The natives will attack a panther with bows and arrows."

He gave the signal and a man led a trained panther on a leash in front of the temple. He let the animal loose and the cameras began to whir. Then, as the big cat slunk toward the jungle, a band of screaming "Mayans" rounded the other

"Look at those sacks," said Holly.

side of the temple. The arrows whizzed through the air.

"Oh, they'll hurt the poor panther!" cried Holly.

The director shook his head and laughed. "They're only blunt arrows with foam rubber on the ends," he said. "They couldn't hurt anybody."

"Look, they're not even falling near the panther," said Pam, trying to comfort her sister.

"Cut!" cried Mr. Grattan.

The camera stopped and the trainer put the collar around the panther's neck again.

"Yikes! That was exciting!" exclaimed Ricky.

But suddenly another arrow zinged through the air. It nicked Uncle Russ's arm and plowed into the ground.

"Oh, Daddy!" cried Jean, racing over to where her father stood, clutching his arm. "That was a real arrow!"

CHAPTER 15

A HIDDEN ENEMY

"I'LL SAY it was!" declared Uncle Russ, while movie people gathered around to see what had happened. The sleeve of the shirt covering the cartoonist's left arm became soaked with red. Teddy rolled it up quickly to reveal a shallow flesh wound made by a sharp arrow.

A crowd of workers gathered around exclaiming excitedly.

"Stand back everybody!" cried Victor Grattan as he pushed his way to Uncle Russ's side.

The director called quickly to an assistant, who rushed up with a first-aid kit. Grattan himself cleaned the wound and bandaged it. He seemed angry that the accident had happened on his motion picture location.

"That arrow was probably meant for me," he said, glancing about the clearing as if to spot any lurking assailant.

"What do you mean?" Pete asked.

"Rivals of ours," said the director, "are out to make trouble for us. This isn't the first time we've had a mishap."

"Yikes," muttered Ricky. He looked around uneasily.

"Do you know your enemies?" spoke up Teddy.

"Not exactly," came the reply.

"Well, I know who they are!" blurted Alexis Regente, the leading actor. "It's John LaPoint."

"Who's he?" asked Pam.

"An agent for Pan Adventure Studios in Hollywood," Regente went on, waving his arms dramatically. "They want to see us fail, because I, Alexis Regente, refused to work on their new picture."

"You can't be sure of that, Alexis," the director said. He turned to Uncle Russ, adding, "Our insurance will cover this accident. I don't think there has been any real harm done."

"The question is," the cartoonist went on, "who shot that arrow?" He bent over, plucked it from the ground, and examined the razor point.

"I saw where it came from," said a gruff voice. Grattan identified the man who had spoken. "This is Mattoon," he said, "one of our grips. What did you see, Joe?"

The man stepped forward. He had curly dark hair and a heavy growth of black beard. "It came from over there, the other side of the clearing," he said.

The Hollisters, along with some of the movie company, walked into the jungle at the spot Mattoon had indicated. The trees were sparse enough for a lurking bowman to have a clear view of the movie location.

"Wait, look!" Pam said, holding her arms out, so that no one would step on the sandy spot before her.

The girl bent down to read some words which had been scratched in the sand. Nearby lay a broken stick. The message read:

"GET OUT OF MEXICO."

"See what I mean?" Grattan spoke up. "My enemies again."

"Maybe not," said Pete. "That might be for us."

"Whoever did it," Regente said, "means business."

Pam glanced at the concerned faces of the people who stood around gazing at the words in the sand. Mattoon, she noticed, was not with them. Looking over her shoulder, she saw the grip hunkered down in the clearing, examining the arrow which had hit Uncle Russ.

"Strange," she thought to herself. "He saw where the arrow came from, yet didn't come here to look around. Isn't he interested in finding out who shot it?"

Pam whispered this to Pete. When they all returned to the clearing, the boy eyed Mattoon, who had laid down the arrow and was nonchalantly flipping a coin with his right hand.

"Tell me," Pete said, "how did you happen to see the arrow coming from the jungle over there?"

Faced by such a blunt question, Mattoon gave a half smile. As he did so, the flipping coin missed his outstretched palm and landed on the ground.

Another plumed serpent coin! It looked identical to the one Pete had found in the rented car at the Shoreham airport!

"Where'd you get that?" Pete asked, bending down to pick up the coin.

Like a shot, Mattoon was on it first. He scooped up the coin and thrust it into his pocket.

"You're full of questions today, aren't you, sonny?" he said. His dark eyes were cold and hard.

Pete could feel his pulse pumping in his ears, and waited a few seconds to regain his composure.

"I'm only curious," he said, trying to hide his excitement.

"One of the natives gave it to me," Mattoon replied. "Said it's a lucky coin, or something like that."

Then the man walked off to help move some large reflectors at the front of the ancient pyramid.

"He could be one of Aguila's gang," said Pam quickly.

"That's my idea, too," said Pete. "The serpent coin might be the insignia the gang members carry."

Pete and Pam quickly beckoned to the cousins and Uncle Russ, then the director and his leading man. Once they were out of earshot of Mattoon, Pete poured out his suspicion that this man might have something to do with their own enemies and perhaps those of the movie company as well.

"Mattoon has been acting sort of strange ever since we came down here," Grattan said in a whisper. "I'll keep an eye on him and let you know any developments."

The Hollisters thanked him, then hastened back through the jungle to the hacienda.

There, Mrs. Hollister and Aunt Marge were shocked to hear of the accident.

"Russ," said Aunt Marge, "there's a physician visiting at this hacienda. I want him to see your wound immediately."

Reluctant to do so, Uncle Russ nevertheless knocked at the door of the physician's room.

Dr. Stein, from New York, a friendly man with hair graying at his temples, said he would be glad to examine the wound.

"It's only a scratch," he said finally. "You're lucky, Mr. Hollister." Then the doctor applied antiseptic and rebandaged the arm.

"Thank you," the cartoonist said. He offered to pay, but Dr. Stein refused, and Uncle Russ said, "I'll give you my card. Perhaps we can meet some day in New York."

He reached for his wallet, then froze. Quickly he patted his pockets. "My wallet—it's gone!"

"Dad, I'll bet it was stolen!" Teddy cried out.

"And I know who did it!" declared Jean. "That Mr. Mattoon from the movie company! He was in the crowd, close to Daddy."

"I'll take care of him right away," Uncle Russ

said angrily. He excused himself from the others, and called on Pete and Teddy to join him.

After a fast trot through the jungle, they reached the clearing in front of the old temple. As Uncle Russ marched sternly up to the director, Mr. Grattan approached him smiling, holding a brown wallet in his hand.

"That's mine!" Uncle Russ said.

"I know," Mr. Grattan replied. "I saw Mattoon searching through it. Then he dropped it and ran. And he'd better not come back here, if he knows what's good for him!"

Russ Hollister took the wallet, looked through it, and groaned. "The map! It's gone!"

"So that was Mattoon's game!" Teddy said. The boy reasoned that in the commotion following his father's accident Mattoon had lifted the wallet. Later he had searched it and removed the map.

"I'll bet he and Punto are buddies!" Pete said.

"Punto?" the director asked, raising his eyebrows. "You know what that means in Spanish?"

"No, what?" asked Pete.

"It means point, Punto—LaPoint, get it? They're one and the same person!"

"Crickets, you're right!" said Pete. He then described the short, dark Mexican whom he had overheard mentioning the name Hollister at the ball court.

"That's him," the director said, snapping his fingers. "Your description fits LaPoint perfectly."

"The map! It's gone!"

"And we're going to find out what's going on," said Uncle Russ. "Thanks, Mr. Grattan." He shook the director's hand, pocketed his wallet, and said good-by.

"Mr. Grattan," Pete put in, "may we come back and do some sleuthing tomorrow?"

"I think not," came the reply. The director said they were using live snakes in the next few scenes. "And we don't want any more sightseers injured," he declared, waving good-by.

When the trio reached the hacienda, they found the local police official talking to the hotel manager.

While Russ Hollister told the news of the arrow and the wallet, the official listened quietly. "All the time trouble with thieves," he said. "First they steal things from the temples and now the crafts shop, and your wallet. I'm very sorry, Mr. Hollister. We'll be on the lookout for this man named Punto or LaPoint."

After the policeman had left, Uncle Russ held a conference with Balám, the women, and the children. They met in the room which he and Aunt Marge occupied. Pete locked the door and they talked in low tones.

"This job is becoming more dangerous than I thought," Uncle Russ told them. "Fortunately Pete has a duplicate of the map, but Mattoon has the one from my wallet!"

"By now Punto and Vargas may have seen it too," Pam reminded him.

"Right," said her uncle. "This means, they'll be on the trail soon, if they're not already carving their way through the jungle toward the Temple of the Laughing Idol."

"Then when will we start?" asked Pam.

Balám had the answer. "I'm afraid the weather will not be good tomorrow. If we meet a storm in the jungle, it would be bad."

"Then what about day after tomorrow?" said Pete.

Balám nodded. "I'll be ready. We will go then." The Mayan asked Pete for his map. "I will study it. Then the map will be here." He touched his head with his forefinger. "Balám will be able to get there, even if the paper should be lost."

After Pete handed it over, the guide said good-by and left the room. Then Jean asked her father, "What if the thief should get to the temple before us?"

"Balám says there's little chance of that," the cartoonist replied. "The jungle is tricky, and he knows of no other native guide willing to penetrate that deeply, especially since the rainy season will soon begin."

Pete went on, "And supposing the thieves *do* get there before we do," he said, "they can't carry the whole temple away in such a short time."

"You're right," Teddy said, brightening. "I never thought of that."

Pam suggested that meanwhile they could still

do some sleuthing around Uxmal. "Maybe we can even help Yotam find what her brother is up to," Holly put in.

"That chicken truck," Teddy declared, "is the key to the whole mystery. If Punto is still driving it, and we could catch him, everything might be solved."

Mrs. Hollister and Aunt Marge thought this was an excellent idea. "But catching that slippery character will be quite a feat," Aunt Marge added.

The meeting over, the youngsters stepped out into the sunshine and lounged by the pool till time for dinner. Afterward the boys entered the manager's office to study a map of the area.

"See here," Teddy said, following a highway, his forefinger on a wall map. "This is the only good road in the area. Punto and that chicken truck of his might pass this way again. Maybe we can find out what he's up to."

"How?" asked Ricky.

"By posting guards on this road," said Teddy. "Then we could follow him."

The boys decided on watches of one hour each. Ricky was first. But it was boring to sit beside the gate and watch. The only thing he saw was an old horse and wagon with a sleepy native man on the high seat. Three Mayan children sat in the back and waved at the boy as the horse clippity-clopped into the distance.

Teddy's watch carried him through until dusk,

and Pete spelled him as darkness settled down over the jungle.

"Ricky might fall asleep on the next watch," said Teddy. "Suppose you and I, Pete, stay up all night and switch every two hours."

Pete agreed to this. While his cousin talked on the portico with the rest of the family, Pete sat with his back against one of the cement pillars of the gateway to watch the road.

Finally two headlights appeared in the distance and a car sped past. Pete settled back again, but did not have to wait long before a familiar sound reached his ears.

The old truck was coming!

Pete rolled over into the shade of a bush and watched. As the truck neared the hacienda, the driver applied more speed. It jangled and jounced along with the crates of squawking chickens piled high.

Pete raced up the drive. "Uncle Russ, hurry! The chicken truck just passed. We can follow it!"

Russ Hollister jumped up. "Come on!" he said. "But not all of you. I can only take four."

"Let the older ones go," said Aunt Marge quickly.

"Aw, yikes," said Ricky as Pete, Pam, Teddy, and Jean ran behind Uncle Russ to the parking lot.

They hopped into the car and soon were zooming along the road. The wind whipped their faces as they peered anxiously into the darkness ahead.

Rounding a curve, they saw a red taillight blinking in the distance. "If he just doesn't suspect us," Uncle Russ said, "we'll find out where he's going."

Mile after mile slipped by beneath the humming tires of the car. The chicken truck kept on without stopping, flashing past little settlements, down the dark road, past the silent jungle.

They neared Mérida, and suddenly the truck's lights veered left.

"Look! He's headed toward the shore," declared Russ Hollister.

The miles droned on. Then the truck suddenly turned left off the road.

"He's getting away!" Teddy cried. "Faster, Dad!"

Uncle Russ increased his speed until he came to the place, then slowed nearly to a stop. "I can't see any side road," he said, squinting into the darkness.

"There it is!" Pam exclaimed. She pointed to a narrow slash among the trees, through which ran two ruts, nearly concealed by underbrush.

"This must be it," said the cartoonist. He drove carefully, with branches and leaves swishing against the sides of the car. All at once they came onto a small sandy cove. Little waves lapped gently onto the shore, and the moon laid a shimmering necklace across the Gulf of Mexico.

Then suddenly out of nowhere, the great beam of a searchlight hit the red sports car with a blinding circle of white!

CHAPTER 16

JUNGLE TREASURE

BLINDED by the glaring searchlight, the Hollisters shielded their eyes, only half able to see a group of men quickly surrounding the red car.

"We are the police!" came a sharp voice. "Get out!"

The leader barked some orders in Spanish, and the searchlight was turned to one side.

When their eyes became accustomed to the semi-darkness again, Uncle Russ and the four children saw that they were surrounded by six police officers.

"You are Americans—right?" the captain said, stepping toward Uncle Russ.

"We are," came his reply. "What's the meaning of this?"

"Show us, where's the contraband?" the chief said, with a note of triumph in his voice.

"The what?" Pete spoke up.

"You know—the antiquities. Precious things from the temples of the Mayans."

As he spoke, several of his men began searching the Hollisters' car.

"You've got the wrong people," said Pam.

"Maybe you're looking for that truck just ahead of us," put in Jean.

"Truck?" said the officer with a frown. "I did not see one, but we've been here only a few minutes."

"Then you missed it," said Pam. "How did you come?"

"Through the jungle," the man replied. The children could now see a narrow lane among the trees. Parked there was a truck with a searchlight on top of it.

As Russ Hollister brought papers from his wallet to prove his identity, the men searching the car reported to their captain in Spanish.

"They say you have no contraband," he said to the Hollisters.

"If there's any to be found," the cartoonist replied, "I'll bet it's in that pickup with the chickens."

"Look!" said Pam. She pointed out over the dark sea, where a tiny yellow light blinked on the horizon.

"Aha!" exclaimed the officer. "That could be their boat, waiting to pick up the stolen goods. I will radio headquarters."

The captain started toward the searchlight truck, but before he had taken three steps, a roar sounded on the road ahead and a glow could be seen beyond the curve.

Suddenly two headlights stabbed through the darkness like the fantastic eyes of a monster!

"It's the chicken truck!" Pete exclaimed.

Quickly the police blocked the road, but the truck careened on, picking up speed.

"Look out!" Teddy shouted. "He's not going to stop!"

"Jump!" yelled Pete. Men and youngsters alike leaped aside as the truck rocketed past. It swerved around the red car and hit the police truck a glancing blow before disappearing down the trail.

Jabbering excitedly, the policemen ran toward their car and tried to call headquarters on their radio. The Hollisters followed, eager to see what would happen.

"It's broken. That bandit destroyed our radio!" the captain said, shaking his fist into the darkness.

"He's your man all right," Teddy called out. "Come here and look at this!"

They hastened to where the boy stood, not far from the red car. There, on the ground, were several crates which had fallen from the truck and broken open. Only one contained chickens, the other two were full of stone carvings. Among the loot was the head of a rain god.

"Just as we thought," the captain said. "Somebody has been robbing the temples and carrying the things to a rendezvous near here."

"And then you mean the boat picks them up?" asked Jean.

"We believe so," replied the officer.

A moment later one of his men called out and pointed to something which he had discovered.

"Jump!" yelled Pete.

Fifty paces farther on lay a sack filled with carvings. Around it were scattered potatoes.

Pete snapped his fingers. "Now I know what's been going on!" he said, and told the police about his sisters seeing boys in the jungle with sacks on their backs. "The potatoes were on top, to conceal the loot underneath, I'll bet."

"Do you know these boys, and where they live?" the policeman asked.

The cousins replied that they did not. "We'll search the jungle for them, though," Pete offered.

"Maybe Tomás would help, so you don't get lost," said Pam.

The chief thanked Pete for his offer and apologized to the Hollisters for thinking they were the thieves.

Then the five Americans got into the red car and headed toward Uxmal. On the way, Pete was silent for a while, thinking hard. Finally he said, "What if Tomás is helping the crooks to carry that stuff off?"

"He comes from such a nice family," said Pam. "If he's doing it, I'm sure he doesn't realize it's wrong."

When they finally arrived at the hacienda, Mrs. Hollister and Aunt Marge were waiting worriedly on the portico.

"Wow! What a night we've had!" exclaimed Pete.

"We almost got arrested!" said Teddy.

"We almost caught the crooks, too," Pam chimed in. Then her uncle reported what had happened.

In the morning before breakfast the older children told the story to the younger ones. When they reached the dining room, they learned that Uncle Russ had already eaten and gone with Balám to report their planned jungle trek to the authorities.

"If they know the area where you'll be," Aunt Marge explained, "help can be sent to you if necessary. Uncle Russ will carry a radio to keep in contact with headquarters."

"Yikes! That gives me the shivers," Ricky said. "Do you think anything will go wrong, Pete?"

"We're up against a rough crowd. Anything can happen."

"Pete," put in Teddy, "we'd better go see Tomás right after breakfast." He mentioned Pete's suspicion.

Holly looked troubled. "I hope Tomás isn't doing something wrong."

"We all hope so," said Pam, and gave the boys directions to the hut where the Ricos lived.

"I would suggest," Mrs. Hollister spoke up, "that you girls spend a quiet day in the crafts shop." Aunt Marge said that Mrs. Rico had a surprise for them.

Taking Sue, the girls skipped over to the shady hut, where the Ricos were busy painting more figurines. "Mother said you have a surprise for us," said Jean, dimpling.

"*Sí, sí,*" The woman put down her work, reached under a counter and brought out a bolt of white material. "We will make *huipils* today," she said. "Pam, Jean, do you know how to cut patterns?"

"Oh, yes," Jean replied. "My mother taught us when we were little."

"Like last year," Pam said, giggling.

While the Hollister girls set about to make Mayan-type dresses, the three boys trotted down to the village back of the hacienda. In the Ricos' yard was a boy busy with a stick and knife, making a bow.

"You're Tomás, aren't you?" Pete said, then introduced himself and his companions.

"Are you going hunting?" Ricky asked.

"When I get this finished," the Mayan boy replied.

"I guess you can find all the wild animals you want here," put in Teddy.

"Plenty of them," came the reply. Tomás said that deep in the jungle lived deer, wild pigs, and even jaguars.

"And what about wild smugglers?" Pete asked.

The question seemed to stun Tomás. He dropped the knife and hastily picked it up again.

Pete walked close to him and said quietly, "We're not going to squeal on you or anything like that, but we have an idea that something funny's going on in the jungle around here."

Tomás continued to whittle while Pete and

Teddy recounted what had happened the night before. The Indian boy's eyes never left the piece of wood in his hand.

Finally Teddy said, "Tomás, your sister is worried you might be in some kind of trouble when you go off into the woods like you do."

"Yotam is wrong," the Indian boy replied, glancing up. "I am not in trouble. But I know—maybe —some people who are."

"Who do you mean?" Ricky asked bluntly.

"They are my friends," Tomás replied. "Every day I go into the forest to see them. They would like to stop what they are doing, but they are afraid. I feel sorry for them," he added.

"Maybe we can help them," said Pete. "If they're carrying loot from the temples, someone must be paying them to do it."

"And those are the really bad ones," said Teddy. "Your friends should tell the police who they are."

"That's the best way out of trouble," Pete added. Tomás did not reply. He kept on whittling, tapering the end of the bow.

"Take us to your friends, Tomás," Pete urged. "Maybe we could convince them to talk."

Just then a small voice from the hut said, "Pete is right," and Tomás spun around.

"Yotam!" he said. "You have been listening!"

"Sí!" his sister replied stoutly. "I have heard. You should let the boys help you!"

Tomás looked from face to face, then said, "All

right. I will go into the forest with you. We will try to find my friends."

"Yo *tam hai*," said Yotam.

This made the Hollister boys laugh, and Yotam's brother said, "No. It might be too dangerous."

"Why don't you go to the crafts shop," Pete suggested, "and help our sisters make *huipils?*"

Yotam's face brightened, and she scooted up the path toward the hacienda.

Tomás beckoned and Pete, Ricky, and Teddy followed him into the jungle. The thick matted treetops nearly blotted out the sun. Only the cries of birds and the hum of insects broke the silence.

Tomás pushed on through bushes and thickets where there was no trail, but finally came to a dimly defined path. Here he stopped, held up his hand, and listened. "I hear," he said.

"I don't," said Ricky.

"Sh!" said Pete.

The four stepped behind trees and waited. Two minutes later a couple of boys came down the trail, carrying empty sacks in their hands.

Tomás stepped out to greet them, but when the Hollisters followed, the young Indians looked frightened. Tomás spoke to them rapidly in the soft language of the Mayans.

The boys shook their heads, glanced about to make sure no one was listening, then dashed on down the trail.

Tomás turned to his companions, and said. "It's no use. They're afraid to go to the police."

"Did you ask who hired them to carry the stuff?" asked Pete.

"Yes," said Tomás. "They will not tell."

"Then let's follow them to see where they're going," Pete suggested.

Quiet as a jaguar on the prowl, Tomás trotted along the jungle path with Pete, Ricky and Teddy following. Now and then he stopped to examine the trail, just to make sure his friends had not gone off in another direction.

After a while the pursuers came to the old railroad track. "Are we near the movie company?" asked Pete. Tomás nodded and Teddy told him that the director had warned them not to go there today.

"That's right, they're going to have dangerous snakes in the scenes," said Ricky.

It was then that Tomás discovered that his two friends had left the trail. Looking carefully for signs of disturbed foliage, the Mayan boy pushed into the thick jungle.

"Are we far from where the movie people are?" asked Pete.

Tomás nodded. "A quarter mile, maybe."

All of a sudden the four boys stopped abruptly and gazed ahead at a small hut cleverly camouflaged by the jungle greenery.

Tomás motioned them to drop to hands and

knees. Then they stalked, like jungle animals, toward the hut.

"Look!" Pete whispered and pointed toward a spot under a tree beside the tiny place. There was a stack of burlap sacks!

Pete was so eager now, that he led the way around the bags to the opening of the hut. With heart pounding, he peered inside the dim shelter.

No one was there. Instead a fantastic stone face met his eye—the head of a rain god! The hut was filled with idols and other carvings from the temples of Yucatán.

CHAPTER 17

A WHOPPER

"CRICKETS!" Pete whispered. "We've discovered the thieves' hiding place."

"Look at all the loot!" exclaimed Ricky.

"What'll we do now?" asked Teddy. "We can't carry all of this stuff away by ourselves."

"We don't have to," said Pete. "We'll notify the police."

As the four boys turned away from the hut, a strange bird call sounded nearby. "That's the same funny one we've heard before," Pete said. "What is that bird, Tomás?"

The Indian boy shrugged. "I do not know."

The thought flashed into Pete's mind that the call might be the thieves' signal. "Come on, fellows," he said, "let's hurry."

It was over an hour later when the four boys returned to the jungle, leading Uncle Russ, Balám, and two policemen.

Hot and sweaty, the party quietly crept up near the hut and stopped to listen before going closer. This time, Pete noted, there was no strange bird call.

Finally one of the policemen stepped from behind a tree and motioned the others to follow him.

He reached the hut, looked inside, then whirled about to face the boys. "You have fooled us!"

The second officer pushed past him into the hut, followed by Uncle Russ. The place was empty except for an iguana, which ran out into the jungle past the dumbfounded boys.

"But-but," Teddy stammered, "the stuff was here a couple of hours ago, honest!"

"Yikes, that's right!" said Ricky while Tomás nodded his head hard.

"The smugglers must have seen you and removed the evidence," his father said.

"I bet I heard their signal," said Pete and told about the bird call.

Balám, who was searching among the trees, called quietly, "I have found a trail."

They all hastened to where the Mayan guide was pointing out trampled underbrush. Single file they followed him along the rough path. About ten minutes later they came out upon the movie location.

"Well, hello there," called out Victor Grattan, seeing the visitors crossing the clearing before the temple. He walked over to them. "If you've come to watch some shooting, we've just finished a scene. Sorry."

"No," said Pete, "we're on the trail of crooks." After introductions had been made, the officers told what had happened.

The director looked surprised. "There were two

men lurking about in the forest," he said. "When several of my men saw them, they hurried off."

"Were they carrying anything on their backs?" asked Teddy.

"Yes. Sacks filled with something heavy. I've told you about these fellows," he added to Russ Hollister. "It was Punto and his tall thin pal. If I see them again, I'll let you know immediately," the director promised. Uncle Russ thanked him, and the party started back to the hacienda.

"I wonder what Punto and Vargas did with all that stuff in the hut," said Teddy.

"Probably hid what they couldn't carry," Pete replied. "The rest will be removed piecemeal."

One of the policemen said that a thorough search would be made for the missing men and carvings. "We will begin as soon as possible." His fellow officer thanked the boys for their help.

When the party reached the village behind the hacienda, Tomás stopped at his house. Pete, Ricky, and Teddy stayed with him while the men went on.

"Thanks for going with us today," said Pete to the Indian boy. "Don't worry about your friends. I have a hunch it won't be long before the crooks are caught."

"We're going on a jungle trip tomorrow," spoke up Ricky, "so we won't see you for a while."

Tomás wished them luck and thanked them for

trying to help his friends. He stood waving as they hurried toward the hacienda.

After lunch, Uncle Russ and Balám summoned all the Hollisters to a shady spot beside the pool, where the two men quietly told their plans for the following day. Everyone was to go except Sue, her mother, and Aunt Marge. Then Uncle Russ brought out a pocket radio and showed the children how to work it.

"I hope you won't need to use that," said Aunt Marge.

The cartoonist smiled. "Don't worry. Balám will take good care of us."

The guide replied that he knew the jungle well, but said the map showed the Temple of the Laughing Idol to be in an extremely dense area which he had not explored before. "But we will get through it," he added cheerfully.

The storm, which had been forecast, struck with sudden fury and dumped tons of water on the forest. As the wind shrieked outside, the boys and men packed their camping gear, while the girls sat in the lobby with their mothers and put the finishing touches on their *huipils*.

"Too bad we won't have time to embroider the tops," said Pam, who was sewing Sue's dress.

"We can always do that later," remarked Holly.

"Perhaps Aunt Marge and I could start the embroidery for you," said Mrs. Hollister.

"I'll 'broider too," piped up Sue.

"That's right. You help us," said Aunt Marge as she gave her littlest niece a squeeze. "It'll give us three something to do while they're searching for the lost temple."

Next morning, after breakfast, the children reported like soldiers to the door of Uncle Russ's room.

Each was issued a small compass and a knapsack with supplies for several days and nights. Pete was given the radio to carry. Between them the men carried tents, cooking utensils, a can of bug spray, and flashlights. In addition, they had long stout ropes slung to their belts.

At the last minute Pam said, "Here's something else." She gave each of the children a small pad and pencil. "Just in case we need them for our code."

With much kissing and hugging, the youngsters said good-by to their mothers and Sue. Then, walking in Indian file, they vanished into the jungle.

Balám was first, followed by Uncle Russ. In a few minutes Ricky scampered up to Balám and said, "May I lead the way for a while?"

"Go ahead. Follow a southwest course."

The redhead, with Pete and Teddy close behind, pushed through the thick foliage until it became too dense to penetrate.

"We're stuck!" Ricky announced.

Balám laughed and pulled a machete from his belt.

Hack! Whack! Thack!

The green vines and broad palm fronds fell to the ground and the hikers pushed into the humid, dark jungle.

Pete and Ricky kept track of the direction and Uncle Russ helped with his machete during the slow trip. Pam and Jean took turns holding Holly by the hand. Uneasily they all looked about for animals. None could be seen, but the strange noises and weird bird calls were proof enough that the forest was alive with wild creatures.

The travelers kept up a steady pace. Now the joking had stopped and even Ricky looked serious. "Yikes! This is like going through a green tunnel!" he said.

The dense underbrush was broken here and there by small clearings of spongy looking rock. At midday Balám came upon one of these places and stopped.

"We rest and eat," he said.

Knapsacks were thrown from damp backs as the Hollister cousins slid to the ground.

"Phew! What a journey," said Pam. "Are you all right, Holly?"

"Yes, but I have short legs," came the reply. "I wish I were grown up like you and Jean."

The youngsters ate quietly, all the while casting glances into the surrounding trees. A snorting sound startled them.

"Just a jungle pig," Balám said. "He'll go away."

When they had finished eating, the girls scattered a few sandwich crumbs around for the wild birds. Then the children wriggled into their knapsacks and started off with Holly and Ricky the last in line.

Hack! Whack! The thud of the machetes sounded as the party moved on again.

They had gone only five minutes when suddenly Holly let out a chilling scream.

Balám whirled around and dashed back to where the girl stood frozen with terror. Uncle Russ followed.

"L-l-look!" Holly stammered and pointed to a tree, where a huge boa constrictor wrapped itself around the trunk. It started to slither to the ground.

Jean gasped and Ricky backed away from the tree.

"Do not be afraid," Balám said. "The boa will not hurt you. It is not poisonous."

"Thank goodness," Pam sighed.

"Crickets! What a whopper," Pete exclaimed. "Wait till I tell the fellows in Shoreham!"

Silently the snake wriggled into the dense jungle and disappeared.

During the rest of the afternoon a few rustling noises and screeching bird calls startled the Hollisters, but they were growing too weary to mind them. For a while Uncle Russ carried Holly on his back. She perched high on top of his knapsack and reached up to slap the overhanging branches.

"L-l-look!"

"Yikes," said Ricky finally, "the temple must be a hundred miles away."

"Getting tired?" Uncle Russ asked.

"Who me?" said Ricky. "'Course not."

The forest grew dark long before the sun had set, and Balám finally called a halt to select a site for their camp. "We've come a long way," he said. "The lost temple should not be far from here. We may find it in the morning."

A clearing had to be hacked in the underbrush before the youngsters could begin setting up their pup tents. Ricky and Holly helped each other drive the pegs into thin soil, and half an hour later the area looked like a little tent city.

Pete and Teddy started a fire, over which they cooked tasty canned stew.

When the meal had been finished, Ricky, Holly, Jean, and Pam crawled into their light sleeping sacks and soon were fast asleep inside their tents.

Pete and Teddy, however, were excited and restless.

"Can't we go a little farther just to look around?" asked Pete.

As Uncle Russ looked doubtful, Balám stood up. "Yes, but I'll follow some distance behind you," he said and smiled. "If you run into trouble, you can yell."

The boys set off, their flashlights showing the way through the heavy brush. Keeping a check on their compasses, they pushed on until they reached a long valley. Standing on the edge, they could look over the treetops which stood out eerily in the moonlight.

Far away on the opposite side, a light flickered. "Hey look at that!" said Teddy. "What do you suppose it is, Pete?"

"Somebody's camping just like us."

"You mean the crooks who are trying to find the lost temple?" asked Teddy excitedly.

"Could be," Pete replied. "Come on, let's hurry back and tell Uncle Russ and Balám."

They met the grown-ups on the trail and told their news. The men looked troubled.

"We can't approach the temple at night," Balám said. "We must wait for sunrise."

"But-but what do we do if we meet those men?" asked Teddy.

"We'll cross that bridge when we get there," Uncle Russ replied.

"From now on I'll keep the radio handy," said Pete. "I'll sleep with it next to my pillow."

The two boys crawled into their pup tents, wondering what the next day would bring.

Thoughts about the lost temple filled Pete's mind as he went to sleep, and the last thing he remembered was a faint bird call.

The next morning Uncle Russ's voice sounded loud and clear. "All right. All of you! Up and at 'em for breakfast!" Sleepy heads emerged from the tents. All except Pete's.

"Hey, come on, get up!" said Teddy, reaching inside his cousin's tent. Suddenly he cried out in alarm. "Hey, Pete, where are you? Look, everybody, Pete's gone!"

The camp was thrown into a turmoil! They called and searched, but there was no sign of the missing boy. Teddy checked Pete's equipment and crawled out of the tent with a piece of paper in his hand. "Dad, look at this. I found a note on his sleeping bag!"

Uncle Russ read the pencil-printed words aloud: "Gone back to hacienda. Meet me there. Pete."

"I don't believe it!" declared Pam. "My brother wouldn't do that. Besides, Pete prints differently."

"That note's a fake!" said Ricky.

"Did you hear anything in the night?" Uncle Russ asked his son.

"Nothing," said Teddy. "And another thing, Dad. The radio's gone too."

"Oh, Pete's been kidnapped!" Pam cried.

Holly started to wail. "Maybe the boa constrictor ate him!"

As Balám calmed the little girl's fears, Jean said, "It must have been the men from the other camp who did it! C'mon, let's get after them right away!"

With drawn and serious faces, the children hastily ate breakfast. Balám, circling around their campsite, found tracks which he was sure had been made by the kidnappers. The trail led parallel to the path made by the boys the evening before when they had seen the light across the jungle.

Quickly the campers packed up and followed Balám along the barely visible path. It led down into the valley, where it seemed to end.

"I've lost the trail," Balám admitted. He squatted down and rubbed his forehead, as if thinking very hard.

"What's next?" Uncle Russ asked.

Teddy spoke up. "Let's head for the place where Pete and I saw those lights. I'll bet the kidnappers took him there."

"Good idea," Balám agreed, and the searchers hurried on. It was midday before they climbed up the other side of the valley.

There they halted for a quick lunch of fruit, rolls, and cheese.

"We're near the place of the lights," Balám said, as they set off once more.

"Everybody quiet now," Uncle Russ warned.

All at once Balám stopped and raised his hand. From the distance came the sound of voices.

The guide whispered, "The map shows the temple to be up ahead. Somebody has discovered it already!"

"I'll fight 'em!" Ricky whispered, clenching his fist.

"And I'll bite 'em," declared Holly.

"Easy now," Uncle Russ said. "Let's be quiet and see what's ahead."

Noiselessly the party pushed through the foliage, parting the bushes carefully with their hands.

The voices grew louder. Somebody was shouting commands, and the sound of flailing machetes filled the air.

All at once the Hollisters peered into a freshly cut clearing.

At least twenty men were hacking on the sides of a crumbling pyramid. Shouting orders at them was Victor Grattan!

The men were so busy they did not notice Balám, Uncle Russ, and the children staring openmouthed at the strange sight. Pam immediately looked about for Pete. He was not there.

All at once one of the workers cut down a huge bush. As it hit the ground, the men let out cries of delight.

There stood the Laughing Idol!

It was partly moss covered and weathered, but still grinning. Behind it the lost temple loomed gray-green and forbidding. Bushes grew out from cracks between the ancient stones. Much of the top of the pyramid had fallen down the sides, which were nearly hidden by the jungle growth.

Balám and Uncle Russ ran into the clearing, followed by the children. "What's going on here, Mr. Grattan?" the cartoonist asked firmly.

The man did not seem to be overly surprised by the visitors. "Oh, hello," he said. "We found a new and better temple for our movie. This one is really ancient."

"That's right," declared Alexis Regente who stood nearby. "This temple is a gem."

"We were supposed to find it first," Holly said hotly.

"Yes, and where's Pete?" exclaimed Pam.

"Wait a minute now. One at a time," Grattan said smiling. "I don't think I understand you."

"How did you find this temple?" asked Balám. Grattan replied that a native had revealed the location of the pyramid.

"And another thing," Uncle Russ said. "My nephew Pete Hollister was kidnapped last night. Do you know anything about that?"

"What? You mean that nice boy with the blond hair?" asked the director. "I'm very sorry to hear it."

"We haven't seen him," Regente spoke up quickly.

"I don't believe anything they say," Pam whispered.

"Neither do I," her Uncle replied.

Trying to hide their suspicion, Uncle Russ, Balám, and the children walked slowly about the ruin. To their surprise they discovered a long, low stone building behind it.

"This must have been a large settlement," Balám said. He told them that the smaller ruin probably had been the residence of Mayan officials. The men walked on ahead.

"And look, there's a big snake again!" said Pam. She pointed at a figure carved in a huge stone slab on one end of the crumbling building.

"It's a boa," said Holly. She and Ricky moved closer to look at the carving. *All at once a small white object fell at their feet.*

Ricky picked it up. "Look," he said, "a stone with a little piece of paper wrapped around it."

"And there's writing on the paper, too," said Holly.

"Yikes!" said Ricky, wrinkling his nose. "A lot of numbers."

Holly's eyes grew wide. "That's our code! It's from Pete!"

Quickly they showed it to Pam and she called Teddy and Jean. The cousins hid behind a palmetto bush and began to figure out the note, which read:

$$\frac{2\,1\,1\,1\ 1}{8\,2\,4\,7\,15}\ \frac{2\ 1\ 2}{8\,15\,7}\ \frac{1\,1\,2\,2\,2\,1\,2}{4\,7\,1\,1\,3\,7\,7}\ \frac{1}{7}\ \frac{2\,2}{3\,8}\ \frac{1\,2}{7\,7}$$

$$\frac{2\ 1\,2\ 1}{1\,2\,2\,1\,15}\ \frac{4\,2\,1\,2}{18\,3\,16\,5}\ \frac{4\,1\,2}{18\,2\,3}$$

Using her code key, the names of the Mayan months, Pam spelled out the message, letter by letter:

mouie men uillain i am in hole back boa

"Of course," said Jean excitedly. "There are no V's in the code so he had to use U."

"There's no S either," said Pam. "So it says: *'movie men villains I am in hole back boa'*."

Pam looked at the stone building and her eyes rested on the carved boa constrictor.

Her brother had been captured by the movie people. He was a prisoner in a hole behind the stone snake!

CHAPTER 18

THE IDOL'S SECRET

THE COUSINS raced from their hiding place to find Uncle Russ and Balám, who were quietly talking on the far side of the pyramid.

"P-Pete's in there!" Ricky whispered, pointing to the low building.

The men were dumbfounded to hear of the discovery, and Balám cautioned everyone not to appear excited.

"We must act as if we know nothing," Uncle Russ whispered. "Now listen to me."

His orders came quickly. Balám, Holly, and Jean were to return to the hacienda for help.

"The rest of us will act as if we're leaving too," the cartoonist said. "But once we're all in the jungle, Pam, Teddy, Ricky, and I will circle back to find Pete."

The Hollisters threaded their way among the workers and approached Grattan.

"Well, I guess Pete isn't here," Uncle Russ said. "We'd better head for the hacienda. And congratulations on your find. I know it'll make a much better movie."

"I hope you find Pete," the director said. "If we can be of any help, let us know."

Waving, the party set off into the jungle. Once among the trees, Balám and the two girls said good-by and hurried away to get the police.

"With a helicopter from Mérida they could be here tomorrow," Uncle Russ said. Careful not to make a sound, he and the remaining three cousins set off Indian file. They circled the clearing and came upon the low ruin from the back.

Stopping at the edge of the jungle, the Hollisters saw the movie men still clearing brush, vines, and twisted trees from the Temple of the Laughing Idol. They were too busy to notice the rescuers creeping toward the old ruin.

Once beneath the boa carving, Pam spoke softly. "How do we get in?"

"There's a stairway to the roof," Teddy pointed out. "Let's try it."

Moving slowly, the four climbed carefully up the narrow crumbling steps.

Uncle Russ reached the top first. He flattened himself and peered over the edge. The workmen had not noticed! The cartoonist motioned to the children. They came crawling on elbows and knees following him toward a square hole in the roof directly in line with the carved boa constrictor! Beside the opening lay a huge flat stone.

In excitement, Pam wriggled past her uncle and reached the hole first. She put her head down into the darkness and whispered loudly, "Pete, are you in there?"

Silence. Pam repeated her question, this time louder.

"Yes, here I am!" came her brother's voice.

Heartbeats thumped in Pam's ears as she relayed the message to Uncle Russ.

"We'll get him," he said. Taking the coil of rope from his belt, Uncle Russ tied one end securely to the heavy stone. As he did so, a bird call sounded at the edge of the woods, but otherwise all was still around the old ruin.

Farther off, the Hollisters could hear Grattan barking orders to his men in front of the temple.

"I'll go down with you," said Pam eagerly.

"We'll all go," said Uncle Russ. "It isn't safe for anyone to stay out in the open." He tested the knot and dropped the rope into the opening. One by one the rescuers slid down into the dim room below.

"Oh Pete!" Pam hugged her brother. "Did Grattan kidnap you?"

"Two of his native workers did. How did you get here?"

"Never mind that now," Uncle Russ whispered impatiently. "Let's all climb out."

But as he spoke, the rope dropped limply at his feet. At the same time a scraping noise startled them. All looked up to see the large flat stone being pushed over the opening on the roof. There was an evil chuckle, then darkness and silence.

Teddy groaned. "I should have known! That bird call we heard! That was their warning signal."

"Somebody must have seen us," Uncle Russ said.

"Yikes. Now we're all prisoners," said Ricky. "How'll we get out?"

They looked about the room, which led to another chamber through a low stone doorway.

The only light came through a crack in the wall.

"I dropped the note through here," said Pete, "when I heard your voices."

"Why didn't you call out?" asked Teddy.

"I was afraid the gang would hear me and we'd all be captured."

"What's in the next room?" Uncle Russ asked.

"Nothing. No windows. No way out."

"What'll they do with us now?" Pam wondered. She looked through the crack in the wall. It was growing dark, and the voices of Grattan and his men faded away.

"I don't imagine they'll do anything with us until tomorrow—if at all," Russ Hollister said gloomily. "Our only hope is in Balám and the police."

The prisoners talked until it became dark. Then they made themselves as comfortable as possible on the dusty stone floor and fell asleep. Ricky awakened first. He looked about the room to see a shaft of sunlight coming through the crack in the wall. It fell on a tiny mound of sand in one corner. The sand moved a little, making a small crater. At once Ricky recognized what it was.

"Look, everybody. A doodlebug!" he called out.

As the rest awakened and stretched sleepily, Ricky got down on hands and knees to observe the bug.

"It's out of sight," the redhead said. With the palm of his hand, he pushed aside the sand to find the doodlebug. Instead his fingers touched the indentations of a carving in the floor.

"Hey, what's this?" The others came to look, and in the strip of sunlight Ricky uncovered a stone face similar to that of the Laughing Idol. But this one was a little different. The open laughing mouth was larger. It was deeper, too. Ricky put his hand inside and found indentations for four fingers. He tried to lift it but the stone was too heavy. Then his uncle bent down, inserted his hand into the mouth of the figure and yanked.

Up came the face of the Laughing Idol!

"Crickets!" Pete exclaimed. "Look down there. It's a secret passageway!"

Below were narrow stone steps leading into a deep dark place.

"You may have discovered how to get us out of here," Uncle Russ said jubilantly to Ricky. "Careful, and follow me."

Hugging the damp, stone wall beside the steps he flicked on his flashlight and led the way down. Ricky was next, followed by Pam and Teddy. Pete brought up the rear. The long stairway finally opened into a tunnel. It was cool and slimy. Water dripped down from the ceiling onto their heads. Uncle Russ stopped and spoke to the children in a hushed whisper. "This seems to be heading toward the old temple."

"Yikes!" exclaimed Ricky. "A secret passageway for the ancient Mayan priests."

"I'm glad they thought of it," said Pam.

"Sh-h-h, not so loud," warned Uncle Russ.

They walked along in silence until Russ Hollister's flashlight played over a stone door.

"Look, an exit!" he exclaimed. All together they pushed and it swung open. The beam shone upon a room that sparkled and danced with reflections from hundreds of gems. Carved gold plates lay on stone tables. Jade necklaces and earrings overflowed from large copper pots.

Uncle Russ sucked in a long breath. "What a discovery! If Skeets could only see this!"

"Crickets!" said Pete, "we'd better get out of here and tell the authorities before Grattan and his crew find this treasure."

On the far side of the room was another flight of steps. The Hollisters climbed quietly out of the treasure vault and found themselves in a second huge stone room. A door on the opposite side revealed a passageway faintly illuminated by light from the outside.

"We must be on the ground level," Pete observed.

"In that case, let's stop here," Uncle Russ advised. "Otherwise we'll run right into Grattan's men."

"What a discovery!" said Uncle Russ.

"I don't hear anybody," Teddy said. They all held their breath and listened intently. Not a sound.

"Maybe they're gone away," Ricky said hopefully.

"Never," Pete disagreed. "They're after the treasure. Maybe they've discovered we got away and are following our trail."

Stand where you are!" Grattan's voice echoed through the chamber, sending icy chills down their backs.

Whirling about, Pete saw three other men with Grattan. One was Regente, the other two were Señor Punto and his friend Vargas.

"Run!" Uncle Russ cried out and the youngsters dashed along the passageway.

"Stop them!" Punto yelled.

But the Hollisters reached the exit and raced into the sunlight with the four men clattering along a few steps behind them.

Outside a group of men awaited them! They all wore uniforms.

"Police!" Pam cried out.

"Police!" Grattan shouted. "Let's get out of here!"

But it was too late. The four thieves were handcuffed and the rest of the gang was rounded up in the treasure room beneath the temple. The officers handcuffed the whole mob and marched them outside.

Once the criminals were herded together, Balám,

holding Holly and Jean by the hand, hastened over to be greeted by the others.

"How did you get help so fast?" Uncle Russ asked, hardly able to believe the whirlwind capture.

"We met the police on the way," the guide said. "Remember? They told us they were going to search the area."

As the police questioned the prisoners about their names, and examined their passports, a strange story unfolded. The movie people were really a gang of treasure hunters who robbed the pyramids.

"All the pictures they were taking are phony," the leader of the police said. "This man Grattan is no more a movie director than a doodlebug!"

Further questioning of the prisoners revealed they had been using innocent boys to carry their loot from the temples to the storage hut. From there it was transported on a fake chicken truck to a place on the seashore, where it was put aboard a boat.

"And to think that Grattan and Regente had us completely fooled," Pam said.

"Not only that," Pete went on, "but Punto and Vargas were in cahoots with them!"

"Vargas and Aguila are the same person," Uncle Russ informed them. "Wow! What a plot for my comic strip!"

Aguila looked sullen. He admitted that Grattan had sent him to Los Angeles to steal the temple map from Skeets. Aguila had eavesdropped when Uncle Russ was getting his instructions from the archeologist. Then he trailed the cartoonist on the airplane to Shoreham and stole the photograph of the Laughing Idol.

"Where did you get that snake you turned loose on the plane?" Ricky asked.

"I brought it with me from Yucatán." Aguila gave an unpleasant grin. "Lots of people are afraid of snakes, so I thought it might be useful."

Balám looked over the prisoners. "This Punto, where is he from?"

"Mexico City," replied one of the policemen. "We checked up on him."

Suddenly Regente said, "Go easy on me! I'll tell you everything!" In a rush of words he told how the gang had tried to get the map showing the location of the temple. Then they did their best to keep the Hollisters from finding the place. "That's why we kidnapped the boy, to lure you back to the hacienda while we robbed the temple."

Pete spoke up. "I'd like you to return my radio and flashlight."

Scowling, Aguila produced both from his pockets. As he did, a small object fell to the ground.

Ricky pounced on it. "The ring I fished out of the cenote!" he shouted.

Grattan's face grew red with anger. "That Aguila! He will steal anything!"

"Look who's talking," sneered Aguila.

"Of course," Uncle Russ put in. "It was Aguila who broke into Skeets's home in the first place."

"And our house too," Holly piped up. "He'll have to get you a new suitcase, Uncle Russ."

While the prisoners argued among themselves, the police went below to examine the treasure room of the old pyramid. They returned to the sunlight, smiling.

"These things will go into our museum in Mexico City," one of the men said. "They are beautiful and perfectly preserved!"

"Here's the ring, too." Ricky handed it to the officer.

Suddenly the sound of a helicopter pierced the jungle stillness.

"Look! A whirlybird!" exclaimed Pam.

With the wind blowing their clothes and hair, the Hollisters watched as the aircraft settled down in a clearing which the thieves had cut from the jungle.

"The copter came from Mérida, as I ordered," the police captain said. "It's to take you Hollisters to Uxmal. We'll march the prisoners back through the jungle."

That evening a party was given in the hacienda to celebrate the return of the heroes. The dining room was decorated with bright-colored flowers, and cake was served with fruit punch.

As the excited guests congratulated the children, Tomás and Yotam stood close by, their eyes shining.

"All right, everybody, quiet please!" called Mr. Cortez. "We want to thank the Hollisters for discovering the Temple of the Laughing Idol and its great treasure, and also for rounding up a gang of thieves."

"There's one more surprise," Mrs. Hollister said. "Come in, Manuel."

The door opened and the bread man entered, balancing the tin and grinning broadly. He walked over to Sue and placed the container on her head.

The little girl's eyes darted left and right to take in the startled glances, before she walked slowly about the room.

The tin balanced perfectly!

"Yikes!" Ricky shouted. "How'd you learn?"

Sue blinked. "While you went to find the pyramid," she said, "Mommy and I practiced!"